THE INDEPENDENT FAIRY

THE INDEPENDENT FAIRY

THE INSCRUTABLE PARIS BEAUFONT™ BOOK 5

SARAH NOFFKE

MICHAEL ANDERLE

DISRUPTIVE IMAGINATION®

LMBPN Publishing
PMB 196, 2540 South Maryland Pkwy
Las Vegas, NV 89109

Version 1.01, July 2021
eBook ISBN: 978-1-64971-890-7
Print ISBN: 978-1-64971-891-4

THE INDEPENDENT FAIRY TEAM

Thanks to the JIT Readers

Diane L. Smith
Veronica Stephan-Miller
Deb Mader
Dorothy Lloyd
Dave Hicks
Zacc Pelter
Jackey Hankard-Brodie

If I've missed anyone, please let me know!

Editor
The Skyhunter Editing Team

To Allen who is definitely one of the coolest guys.

— Sarah

*To Family, Friends and
Those Who Love
to Read.
May We All Enjoy Grace
to Live the Life We Are
Called.*

— Michael

The jail smelled musty with a sickly saccharine odor overlaid and was cold, reminding Agent Ruby of his youth. He snarled, holding an embroidered handkerchief to his mouth and nose that read JPW.

The initials stood for John Paul Williams. That had been Agent Ruby's name before he attained the position of an agent at the FGA. Now John Paul Williams was all but dead to him. He was now the man who wielded the silver ballpoint pen with a red ruby at its end as his magical instrument.

His magic was full of the tracing substance of the ruby gem, and he was a powerful agent for the Fairy Godmother Agency—ruling over fairy godmothers to create elite matches. There was only one other name that Agent Ruby ever wanted, and that was Saint Valentine. To get that title, he only needed to take out one man—the reigning ruler of the fairy godmothers.

Everyone knew that each agent's magic was traceable to their gem, which was why tying Agent Topaz to the murder of Agent Opal had been quite easy. All he had to do was steal his pocket watch—his trademark magical instrument—which had his tracer: the purple topaz. Then he used it to create the poison to kill Agent Opal...which he'd intended for Saint Valentine. Still, everything had almost worked.

Agent Ruby had nearly killed the reigning leader of the fairy godmothers. He'd also deflected a lot of heat off himself from those growing suspicious. Now they all looked at Agent Topaz and not at him when things didn't go as suspected at the agency. Plus, Agent Ruby had nearly put all the blame on Paris Beaufont.

She was his biggest problem.

Unnoticed by the guards, Agent Ruby blazed through the outer corridors of the jail around FLEA, formally known as Fairy Law Enforcement Agency. The uniformed guards might have felt a brush of wind or heard the scuff of Agent Ruby's soft-soled shoes, but that was about all as he passed right beside them, seemingly in plain sight but invisible.

He was there, yet strange and powerful magic he'd only recently tapped into hid him. However, to get the full extent of the magic's capabilities, Agent Ruby would need to put a lot more things in place, and that would take time. All of those measures were necessary to cover his tracks. His greatest concern was taking out the one man who could tell his secrets and put the interrogation light on him.

Agent Ruby paused outside the locked corridor that led to the jail cell where FLEA held Agent Topaz before his trial. He was the only one who could give testimony that would indict Agent Ruby for the murder of Saint Valentine's agent. If that man started talking, everything could fall apart—everything that Agent Ruby had worked for.

He hadn't worked his way up the ranks of the Fairy Godmother Agency to see it taken over by a liberal Saint Valentine who entertained the idea of allowing commoners to marry royalty. No, Agent Ruby had always seen his mission was clear. Born from pure fairies of an ancient lineage, he knew that the only way to protect where he came from was to preserve the ways of tradition. However, the old values were vanishing in the modern world, and Agent Ruby had sat back for too long.

First, he'd take out the only one who could indict him for the murder of Agent Opal.

Then he'd further ruin the current Saint Valentine's reputation, which was already crumbling in the eyes of the board. The love meter might have recovered when the fairy godmothers took FriendNet down, all thanks to the meddling of Paris Beaufont. He'd deal with her in time though. However, Agent Ruby already had new plans to bring the love meter to zero since the godmothers foiled his last attempt.

First, Agent Ruby would cover his tracks. Then he'd work to take down Saint Valentine. Other ways besides social media could ruin love and make the current leader of FGA look bad, all while using things that Saint Valentine supported, like technology, for instance. That would surely make Saint Valentine look incompetent, and before too long, the board would vote him out of office.

Agent Ruby mischievously chuckled as he removed an object from the inside of his black suit jacket pocket. The thought that phones—a modern convenience supported by the current Saint Valentine and the leader of the fairy godmothers—would be his very demise was extremely satisfying. All Agent Ruby wanted was to take down this fickle leader who had risen through the ranks and taken over to rule with his wrong ways and untraditional ideas. Then Agent Ruby could do what he wanted with the college and the agency, leading it the way he saw fit.

First, though, he had to cover his trail.

Second, he had to take down Saint Valentine.

Last, he had to rid the college of the most startling evil...Paris Beaufont.

The last part would prove most troublesome, but he wouldn't stop until the halfling was out of his way.

Agent Ruby placed a small mirror in the corner of the corridor. It attached to the wall easily. Most wouldn't notice it, and the best part was that in time, it would ensure that *he* went unnoticed further into the jail area where the magical wards were higher than at his present position.

The man who was once John Paul Williams was only a few steps away from taking the position away from the current Saint Valentine.

Then he could rule love the way it should be: reserved for the few who deserved it.

CHAPTER TWO

"I did a lot of experiments." Faraday continued to rustle around in the sock drawer of the dresser in Paris' room.

"What kinds of experiments?" Paris asked pointedly.

"All kinds."

"What kinds?" she asked again.

He shook his head. "I don't know how to explain them, but they were unimportant."

Paris got the distinct impression that Faraday was telling her something she didn't know about him without telling her. He was proving to be an enigma as he opened up.

Like, was he unhappy with his life before or happy with his accomplishments? She didn't know, but she was going to find out.

"What was your life like?" She combed her hair away from her face as she regarded herself in the mirror above her vanity at fairy godmother college. "You know, when you were…you know…"

"A man," he supplied.

She nodded. "Yeah, that."

It was still weird to think that at one point, before the experiments with Edison and Curie and the magic and time traveling, that Faraday had been a man. Harder still was the idea that when given a choice, he'd decided to stay a squirrel instead of a man in his timeline, returning to his old life. However, that's what he'd wanted. A life with Paris as a rodent was apparently better than one standing upright with the ability to vote and be and do all that humans could. She still couldn't understand it, but she was trying.

"I know it seems strange to you that I decided not to go back," he said on the heels of her thoughts, almost as if he could sense them. "You have to understand that I didn't have a life as Faraday the man. I loved my work, and that was about it. I had…no one. No life. Nothing outside of science. Then I got stuck as a squirrel, and I met you and everything in my life—well, it has been different ever since. Better."

"It does seem strange," she had to admit. She chewed on her lip and looked at the squirrel in the mirror over her shoulder.

"It would to you." He looked out the window to the Enchanted Grounds where the sun rose over another day at Happily Ever After College.

"Why?" She turned to look at the talking squirrel directly.

"Because you don't know what it's like to be with you."

Her mouth dropped open. "What a weird thing to say."

"Well, it's true," he argued, seeming offended. "You change those around you. I don't think you realize it. Just by being you, you make those around you happier. You make people feel accepted."

Paris was suddenly silent. She didn't know how to respond. Telling Faraday that he was going senile seemed like the best approach, but that probably wasn't the right thing to say. Instead, she tucked her chin to her chest. "When you were Faraday the man, you were lonely."

He nodded. "But all the searching in the world didn't help. It wasn't until I met you and your life that I found what I was looking for. Society tells you that you need this or that, but the truth is that the right fit for each is different. You fit my life and make sense to me, Paris. I know it seems weird that I want to stay a squirrel, but it simplifies my life and allows me to be less complicated so I can think about that which is more complicated."

"Like science," she guessed.

"Exactly," he answered with enthusiasm. "I'm not sure if you realized, but your life is rather extraordinary to witness."

"Because I'm a blonde who knows how to do complex math?" she deadpanned.

He nodded with a twinkle in his eyes. "As well as being the first and only halfling magician fairy we know about, born to Warriors for the House of Fourteen with demon blood."

She faked a yawn. "I think it's more interesting that I once came in thirty-sixth in a trivia game at Sullivan's Bar and Tavern."

"That is quite impressive," he chirped.

"There were, like, fifty contestants," she added, straightening her leather jacket.

"Leave that part out," he offered and nudged her phone over on the top of the dresser. "I think it's ready."

Paris' mouth popped open again. "Are you serious?"

"Well, it's not any trivia prize," he muttered shyly. "But I think I enabled your phone so that it has data capabilities as well as gets messages at Happily Ever After College."

She snatched up her phone. "Which makes me the only one here with that option. You're brilliant."

He batted his eyes, embarrassed. "I don't know about that."

Paris regarded the squirrel. "What do you need to feel accomplished? A Nobel Prize?"

Faraday shook his head. "Nothing I've done is quite so noteworthy. I like to dabble in science. It's nothing extraordinary."

Paris smiled at her friend. "You think I'm extraordinary and somehow, I'm going to convince you that you are too."

He shook his head. "I've never done anything of any great value. That's the key for a scientist to make their mark. I'm curious, and it has led to discoveries, but only that. Nothing of any real worth to the real world."

Paris swelled with pride, but she didn't know why. Something told her this was the beginning of a moment. One that hopefully she could look back at and point to as a precursor to something bigger. She liked those kinds of moments. They felt bigger than the monumental ones. "Well, maybe Faraday the squirrel has things to do that will change the world. I think he already has, but it sounds like he has to prove it to himself first."

Faraday glanced back at her, turning his attention away from the glowing Enchanted Grounds. "I don't have anything to prove to me. I'm hoping that you keep me around."

Paris wanted to laugh. "Of course I'm keeping you around." She held up her phone. "I get to look up random stuff on the Internet again, thanks to you."

"I put on parental restrictions," he admitted.

"Why?" She was suddenly offended.

"Because there are bad things out there in the world."

Paris lowered her phone. "*I'm* those bad things."

He nodded. "I don't want you out there causing problems for the innocent."

She nodded and pocketed her phone. "What are you doing today?"

Faraday returned his attention to the window. "I'll let my curiosity lead the way."

"So where should I go to rescue you later then?" she teased.

He shook his head. "You have enough troubles with researching Agent Ruby and whatever he's after and all the rest. I'll try not to be a bother for you."

Paris nodded, making for the door, her stomach ready for some of Chef Ash's hearty breakfast. "I do have a mission on top of a mission with my regular school work. Try and have fun on your adventures."

Faraday hopped onto the window sill, his tail flicking. "Thanks. Try and stay out of trouble yourself, although I get that's a lot to ask for."

Paris chuckled, opening the door. "Where would the fun in that be?"

The squirrel flashed her a grin. "It definitely wouldn't be your style. Call me if you need a hand—or a paw, as it were."

"Always." Paris headed out the door, grateful that she had a partner in...well, hopefully putting crime to bed.

CHAPTER THREE

"Bacon is the best thing ever invented." Christine crammed a thick strip of maple bacon into her mouth and hardly chewed as she gobbled it down.

Paris shook her head, tearing into a buttery croissant. "Wrong. Bread is the best thing invented. It is nothing without carbs."

Christine lowered her chin, regarding Paris from across the table as if she'd said something rather offensive. "It's things like that which make everyone question your judgment. No wonder you're constantly the talk of this place."

The group all laughed.

"I think that's more because she's half-fairy and half-magician and was outed as having demon blood," Hemingway offered through a bite.

"Not to mention that rumors are spreading that you have a pet squirrel who can talk," Chef Ash commented.

"And fix computers," Christine added. "I got a nasty virus on my laptop, and Faraday offered to look at it."

"Maybe stay off the free poker sites," Hemingway suggested. "They're full of stuff that corrupts."

"You'd know," Christine sang. "No, I use my computer for typing up my assignments. I wish I could get onto websites at the college, but it's locked down tighter than a bullfrog's behind."

"I'm not aware of how tight that is." Chef Ash buttered his muffin.

"Tight," Christine answered with certainty.

Paris glanced at her phone sitting on the table beside her plate. "Well, maybe he can help you with that. Faraday somehow managed to get data on my phone."

Christine's fork clattered loudly to her plate, making many around them look up. "Are you serious? You get a talking squirrel as a sidekick—"

"Who tears up all my socks," Paris cut in.

"Badass parents," Christine continued, ticking off a second finger as though making a list.

"Who no one can know have returned to the world yet," Paris added.

"And an aunt who is a dragonrider," Christine stated, holding up a third finger.

All eyes looked at Paris as though expecting her to reply with a con. She shrugged. "Sophia Beaufont is pretty cool. There's no denying that, although her dragon tells the worst jokes."

Christine sighed dramatically and slid down in her chair. "Do you want to know what my aunt does for a living?"

"You're going to tell us regardless," Hemingway muttered. He pushed his food around on his plate with this fork, seemingly looking for something under the eggs and hash browns.

"She works in quality management services in the Pegasus corrections office, reviewing learning outcomes for modifications in their behavioral therapy program," Christine stated.

"That sounds interesting." Penny Pullman joined the conversation, although she'd been listening intently as usual on the sidelines.

Christine shook her head. "It means she reviews spreadsheets all day. I can't explain all this to you without getting sleepy. Spreadsheets. Meanwhile, Paris' aunt is gallivanting off on majestic dragons named Caspian the Great and saving the world."

"Lunis," Paris corrected. "But yes, to saving the world. I can't argue with that."

Christine threw her head back. "It's not fair. When there's a rumor, it's always about you. 'Who is the first magical halfling in all of history?' 'Paris Beaufont.' 'Who saved the love meter?' 'Paris Beaufont.' 'Who killed that guy from FriendNet?' 'Paris Beaufont—'"

"I didn't kill Dash," Paris interrupted.

Ignoring her, Christine continued, seeming locked in her world as she stared at the ceiling. "'Who killed Agent Opal?' 'I bet it was that halfling with the demon blood.'"

"I hope you corrected whoever rumored that." Chef Ash sipped his coffee.

Christine sighed. "What's the point? Then these gabbing girls were like, 'Did you see that handsome guy who carted Agent Topaz away for the murder of Agent Opal? I heard it was Paris Beaufont's uncle. He's so dreamy.'"

Paris laughed at the idea that Uncle John was considered dreamy. She guessed that to others he had a sophisticated look. "I'm still not convinced it was Agent Topaz," she whispered, conscious that Becky Montgomery was sitting close by and always snooping.

Chef Ash shook his head. "It's pretty much an open-and-shut case, I'm afraid. If they found topaz laced into the potion that created the poison that killed Agent Opal, then we have our killer."

"As if someone can't have gotten hold of that gem and used it to frame Agent Topaz," Paris argued quietly.

"I'm afraid it's not that easy," he replied. "There will be a unique brand of topaz linked to the agent's magical instrument. It's only a matter of proving that it came from his pocket watch. Then the whole thing is signed, sealed, and delivered."

"Someone could have stolen his pocket watch," Paris countered.

Hemingway shook his head at this. "You don't understand. Fairies, especially agents, don't leave their magical instruments lying around. It would have been difficult for someone to take Agent Topaz's pocket watch and use it."

"Difficult, but not impossible." Paris leaned forward, her head low.

"I'm telling you, I saw Agent Ruby with a silver ballpoint pen as Dash at FriendNet described. He's the one who orchestrated that whole debacle."

"So he went to FriendNet." Chef Ash shrugged. "He could have had several reasons. Maybe he was starting to get suspicious about the social media company before things went haywire. He could have been on the cusp of figuring things out before you did."

Paris shook her head. "I don't think so. I think he's behind it." She looked around the dining room, which was starting to empty as students made their way to their first classes of the day.

Since Agent Opal's murder and Agent Topaz's subsequent removal, the other agents from FGA had left the college, making it feel more normal once more. "Something tells me that man is behind all this. I can't prove it, but I'm not going to rest until I get to the bottom of it."

Hemingway stood, staring down at Paris with a soft smile. "Well, in between trying to solve mysteries and all, try and focus on your magical gardening studies. There's a test coming up."

Chef Ash joined him, stretching to a standing position. "While you're at it, ensure you memorized all the magical herbs in your textbook. I heard there might be a pop quiz today in Magical Cooking and Baking."

"Man, that professor is a real jerk," Christine joked, dramatically sighing.

"The very worst," Chef Ash agreed with a wink.

Paris let out a breath, not worried about her upcoming quizzes, which she thought she'd ace without studying for, although she wouldn't tell Christine that. Her friend had to work hard to retain information, much like most fairies. Thankfully they were pretty, which made up for their lack of brains. And also, mostly very loving.

The frustrating thing about FriendNet was that all the information about the corruption it had done to relationships had been wiped clean after Dash's death. It was almost as though someone had known and covered it up before FLEA could investigate.

Now Saint Valentine's office, Matters of the Heart, was calling the whole thing a fluke of frustration created by a bitter hipster who was working alone. Paris knew better. She knew that Agent Ruby was behind it. She had to find proof.

Somehow, she believed it would also link him to the murder of Agent Opal, but proving that would take a lot of work. Thankfully she had time to devote since she didn't have to study for her upcoming tests.

CHAPTER FOUR

Paris wasn't sure what Faraday had done to her phone. She thought he'd enabled it to allow data, but it felt different somehow—like it was constantly calling to her, demanding her attention. As she sat in Art of Love class, waiting for the professor to arrive, Paris could hardly pull her gaze away from the device.

She suddenly felt like an addict, needing to check her email, updates on social media sites, news, and anything else she could access with her phone. It was strange and unexpected. Paris didn't know why she had this new obsession. It wasn't like she was an addict to it before she had data. She'd only had Faraday enable it so she could do research more easily. Now, she felt as if she wasn't looking at her phone, scrolling through options, checking on things, that she was incomplete.

Something wasn't right, and she knew it deep in her core.

Forcing herself with every fiber of her being, Paris put the phone in her leather jacket's pocket as Headmistress Willow Starr strode into the classroom. Paris was grateful to see the fairy godmother in her long blue gown with its pink ribbon around the collar and grayish-blue hair pinned into a neat bun on top of her head. If she was in the classroom, that meant an uptight FGA agent wouldn't be teaching Art of Love. Hopefully, things would return to normal, although Paris couldn't convince herself of that entirely.

Agent Topaz might stand accused of trying to murder Saint Valentine, but the fact remained that there was conflict among the ranks in the Fairy Godmother Agency. It had been growing for quite some time, according to Headmistress Starr. The board was constantly critiquing the way the current leader of the fairy godmothers did things. The attempt on Saint Valentine's life seemed like only a result of more problems that might follow. There was a divide between the old ways and the new at FGA, and it was constantly growing wider.

"You all were assigned to read part of an untraditional book for today's lesson," Headmistress Starr began, turning to the class with a light smile. She held up a rather worn hardback book. *Zen and the Art of Motorcycle Maintenance* is—"

"Not a story about love," Becky Montgomery interrupted. "Mother says that it's a travesty to subject us to such literature and that the board is questioning why this is assigned reading."

Paris sighed, wondering if she should pop the fairy in the face first or tell her off before that. She let out a breath, quelling her urge toward violence.

Headmistress Starr, ever the picture of poise and patience, smiled politely. "Rebecca, although I understand that this isn't the usual curriculum you're used to studying in this class, I contend that it holds merit for your education as a fairy godmother. Under the current administration of Matters of the Heart, we are encouraged to use materials that are outside our previous range of subjects."

Willow's eyes briefly connected with Paris before returning to Becky. "Saint Valentine has said to be inspired by a different way of approaching love that will be more fitting for the modern world. I think this book gives us a different perspective that we hadn't considered before when only studying purely traditional romantic literature."

"We shall see how long this push for new curriculum lasts," Becky remarked, a hint of a threat in her voice. "My family has made their position on this quite clearly known to the board."

Paris couldn't take it any longer. Based on the look on Willow's face, she knew that Paris had hit her threshold. The fairy godmother sighed, seemingly resigned to what was inevitably going to happen next.

Spinning around in her chair, Paris scowled at Becky Montgomery, who wore the blue gown uniform, the same as everyone else and also a hostile glare. "You do realize no one cares that your family seems to think they run this place, right?"

"Actually, my family does have a strong influence over Happily Ever After College," Becky fired back. "My mother advises the board often and is in the know when it comes to what's happening behind the scenes at FGA. For that reason, I know that Saint Valentine's rule is very much under question, and taking his advice to use a different range of learning materials isn't something that's required at this point and probably not a good idea."

Paris narrowed her eyes. "How very bold of you to question the headmistress' judgment directly in front of her. I thought your usual style was to badmouth people behind their backs."

Becky's gaze narrowed as well on Paris. "Following the advice of a man the board is heavily scrutinizing is questionable."

"You know, it doesn't sound like you approve of Saint Valentine very much," Paris replied, a mischievous quality to her tone.

"Many don't," Becky fired back.

"Another bold choice, admitting to not liking a man someone nearly murdered recently." A sideways smile flashed on Paris' face.

Becky gasped and pressed her hands to her chest, offense written in her every action. "How dare you insinuate such a thing. I didn't have anything to do with that. Everyone knows that Agent Topaz was behind that unfortunate incident."

"No, he's on trial," Paris corrected. "We're not to convict people of crimes until they've had a trial, you realize, right? There are laws although I'm sure the Montgomerys don't think they apply to them. Since you're so helpful, saying that many don't like the current leader of FGA, I think that means there could be others who wanted him dead."

Becky scoffed loudly. "My family may not agree with how Saint Valentine is ruling, but we'd never condone murder."

All eyes in the classroom turned to Paris, wondering how she'd reply to this. Becky was visibly flustered, her freckled face flushed pink with frustration. "No, you make threats and publicly voice your disapproval about how the college is managed." Her typical sarcasm made an appearance when she added, "You're definitely not stoking a fire that creates more divide rather than helps the FGA to come together during this time of unrest."

"Are we supposed to sit back and watch as centuries of tradition wash down the drain?" Becky nearly yelled, her anger evident.

Paris remained calm, turning back to face the front of the class. To her surprise, Willow also appeared rather at peace despite the current argument going on in her class. "No, you should hold on fervently to the old ways that don't work and are supposed to create love for the few instead of trying to evolve in a world that's ever-changing."

Becky sounded like she jumped to her feet. She stomped down the center row and arrived in front of Paris' desk, shaking with anger. "You know nothing about FGA or this college and how it should run. New isn't better. Our services are for royalty. We aren't to waste our time on commoners. Their relationships have little effect on the world, and if you knew anything, you'd know that."

Paris blinked at Becky, hiding the glee that she'd flustered her so much. She calmly glanced at Willow. "Sorry for the interruption, Headmistress Starr. I'd love to discuss *Zen and the Art of Motorcycle Maintenance*."

"No!" Becky exclaimed, her fist balled up by her side. "We aren't done talking about this."

"I've finished," Paris sang casually, smiling at Willow, who also seemed to be hiding her satisfaction over how this was all playing out. Becky losing her temper was making her look unprofessional and irrational, whereas Paris was the picture of confidence.

"You can't start an argument and be done when you want!" Becky yelled, shaking her head erratically.

"Well, of course, I can," Paris stated. "We aren't arguing. You made a threat, and I told you that no one gives a damn."

The curse word seemed to fluster Becky more. "We are arguing. And I'm right. You're backing down because you know I am. Saint Valentine is ruining the integrity of FGA. I can prove it."

Paris yawned. "I don't care. Also, I refuse to argue with you."

"Because you know I'm right!" Becky stuck her shaking hands on her hips.

Paris shook her head and glanced at Christine beside her as if they had been having a conversation. "As Mark Twain said, 'never argue with a fool, because onlookers may not be able to tell the difference.'"

At this, the class erupted with nervous laughter. Christine's reaction was anything but nervous as she slapped the surface of her desk. Willow appeared to be having trouble restraining a grin.

Becky looked on the verge of crying as she stormed from the classroom, her long hair catching as she ran for the door, muttering a series of hostile words.

CHAPTER FIVE

"Some people are such drama queens," Christine sang when the laughter in the classroom had died.

Willow drew in a breath, relaxing a little with Becky gone from the room. "I do apologize for that interruption. I think that it would be unwise to ignore the fact that some don't approve of some of the curriculum changes we're entertaining at Happily Ever After College or that Saint Valentine doesn't have the full support of the FGA board. I encourage all to voice their opinions in productive ways, but at the end of the day, I'm the headmistress of this college and will run things the way I see fit, regardless of what donors and alumni think."

Paris smiled proudly at Willow, glad that she showed such calm confidence and stood by her principles. She knew it wasn't easy for the headmistress to take this stance when so many were casting judgmental eyes on her. Still, she had proven to be open to what was best for the college, rather than simply doing what the old families advised and approved of.

"I think you're doing an excellent job of trying to balance new ways with the old traditions," Penny said from the other side of the classroom.

Willow smiled with gratitude and nodded. "Thank you. Your endorsement means a lot."

Unfortunately, Paris knew that Penny's endorsement didn't have the same weight as the Montgomery family. They were powerful and had a lot of influence due to their money and various positions. Conversely, Penny was on a scholarship at Happily Ever After College. She didn't come from an affluent family.

Christine waved. "Not to change the subject or anything, but did anyone else want to buy a motorcycle after reading our assigned book?"

Many in the class laughed, further breaking the tension.

Willow appeared grateful for this, allowing her to change the subject easily and return the topic to that day's lesson. "Many are surprised that *Zen and the Art of Motorcycle Maintenance* has little to do with mechanics and much to do with one's worldly approach to love."

"I thought it was interesting the way the narrator turns something as seemingly unartful as motorcycle repairs as the metaphor for one's attitude toward the world," a student offered.

Willow nodded. "Yes, and the main character's approach versus that of his friend's creates a nice dichotomy. For our purposes of studying love, what did you all find most interesting?"

Christine tapped the open paperback sitting in front of her. "Here's a quote that's pretty apropos based on the scene we all witnessed." She glanced down at a highlighted section and read, "You are never dedicated to something you have complete confidence in. No one is fanatically shouting that the sun is going to rise tomorrow. They *know* it's going to rise tomorrow. When people are fanatically dedicated to political or religious faiths or any other kinds of dogmas or goals, it's always because these dogmas or goals are in doubt."

Paris was glad it was her friend and not her who had made this point. It was true that the more Becky tried to argue and make her case, the more it sounded like she was trying to convince herself of her reasons.

"Thanks for that," Willow said with a calm expression. "It's true that doubts lead one to try and make a case whereas those with confidence often aren't compelled to persuade anyone of their side."

"I think for our purposes as fairy godmothers," Paris began, "we should consider using both a romantic and analytical approach when creating love. That was the takeaway in the end, right?"

Willow nodded. "Indeed, it was. Remember that the author, Robert M. Pirsig, talks about artists and scientists and the real dilemma that they face."

"Yes," Paris affirmed, glancing at the cover of the paperback lying in front of her. "He said, 'We have artists with no scientific knowledge and scientists with no artistic knowledge and both with no spiritual sense of gravity at all, and the result is not only bad, it is ghastly.'"

"Did you freaking recite that from the book from memory?" Christine gawked at her.

Paris shrugged. "It was a good line. I remembered it."

Christine rolled her eyes. "Remembered it. So not fair. Do you know how long it took me to read this book? And you're over there reciting it from memory."

Willow offered a sympathetic smile. "Magicians are very skilled in computational skills as well as retention."

"Is there anything this girl can't do?" Christine asked.

"I can't outdrink a gnome," Paris joked. "I've tried. Those guys can hold their liquor better than any other creature."

The class laughed although Paris also heard a great many whispers behind her. A fairy godmother getting drunk with a gnome was not typical behavior. However, Willow didn't seem too put off by the statement.

"The quote you recited reminds us of our purpose for this lesson." Willow smiled at Paris. "I think the fairy godmothers have focused on romance without reason for too long. Our current Saint Valentine has taken effort and risked reputation to get us to see that a rational approach to love is worthwhile.

"That's the reason I chose this book. We don't have to be what we've been. We, as fairies and matchmakers, can choose to be something new, something better. And for the chief reason of having greater success."

Willow's gaze revolved around the room briefly before she spoke again. "Yes, the love meter is currently low. It's dipped many times lately. I have to believe that's because we are resetting our ways, ideals, and power structures. We all want the same thing: love. But how we get there needs to be strategic.

"I believe that we are finally starting to think in ways that will work for all rather than some. We are looking for effective ways that will benefit many. I want to believe that the fairy godmothers are evolving in great ways, but to some, change looks like regression. To some, change looks like we're losing our ways instead of gaining new ones."

The room was quiet for a moment, many contemplating the deep messages delivered by the headmistress. Finally, Willow said, "Let's remember what the author of *Zen and the Art of Motorcycle Maintenance* said about improving and take it to heart when individually deciding how to proceed. Remember, we only change the world when we change ourselves. Robert M. Pirsig said, 'The place to improve the world is first in one's own heart and head and hands, and then work outward from there.'"

CHAPTER SIX

"To be able to dance is more than knowing the moves," Wilfred, the magitech AI butler began, addressing the class from the front of the ballroom in Fairy Godmother Mansion.

An odd fellow who Paris didn't recognize was standing next to Wilfred. He had a long silver beard and a curious gaze as he regarded the students all standing at attention. Beside him was a large traveling chest that no doubt was full of magic.

"You need music," a student with a hippie name like Honey or Rebel offered.

Wilfred nodded. "Correct. Music is a must for dancing."

"You need grace," someone else offered.

"That doesn't hurt," Wilfred stated.

"You need a hot pair of dancing shoes," Christine sang.

"Exactly the answer I was looking for," Wilfred said proudly.

"It was?" Christine asked, surprised. "I was joking."

Paris leaned over and whispered. "Wilfred doesn't do jokes, but I'm working on him. I've deduced which jokes don't work."

"Which are?" Christine asked.

"All of them." Paris giggled.

Christine studied the butler who was going on about appearance and style for some odd reason. "It's going to be something unexpected that makes the AI laugh. Like slapstick or maybe a dirty joke."

Paris glanced at her friend with a skeptical expression. "I don't think so. Wilfred Biltmore is the epitome of refinement."

"Those are the ones who will surprise you most," Christine offered. "I bet if he got to become a real man, on the weekends, he'd sit in his underwear on the sofa watching trash television while eating cheese puffs."

Paris covered a laugh, trying not to get in trouble for talking while Wilfred went on about fabrics and fashion, again for whatever bizarre reason. "I think you're projecting onto the butler. That sounds like your perfect weekend."

Christine nodded. "I've been known to have Dorito dinners and marathon an entire season of *Real Housewives* over a weekend. Some crave adventure and sunshine on their days off. I want to lick cheese dust off my fingertips and gawk at the idiocy of humanity. Is that too much to ask?"

Paris shook her head, stifling her amusement. "It isn't. I think it needs to be you who tries to get Wilfred to laugh. You have a better chance than me."

Christine pursed her lips. "Oh, no. I'm only funny by accident. Again, humor isn't something that comes easy to fairies. About like understanding simple math. Comedy requires intelligence, and Mother Nature apparently thought it was better if we were cute rather than comedians."

"I didn't think the two had to be mutually exclusive."

"They usually are, with you being the exception, which again is totally unfair," Christine huffed.

"Today, we won't be doing any dancing," Wilfred said, getting Paris' attention.

"Yes," she said under her breath, wanting to fist-bump her friend out of sudden excitement. She refrained.

"Instead, you all will undergo fittings for your formal ballroom gowns," Wilfred continued.

"Say what?" Paris nearly exclaimed, gaining the attention of everyone in the room.

Wilfred nodded calmly. The man beside him tilted his head, surprised by her sudden outburst. Hemingway, who had been fixing some flooring in the corner, stuck his hand to his face, obviously embarrassed for Paris.

"As I had been saying," Wilfred continued. "A dance isn't complete unless one is elegantly dressed."

"I don't agree," Paris countered, wishing she hadn't missed what the butler had been saying. "We need music, dance moves, and shoes, I guess. But needing a dress to dance is like saying that you need a fork to eat."

"I would contend that you do," Wilfred argued.

"You don't," Paris stated with confidence. "It might make it easier, but what if it's a burger? Then a fork would make it harder to eat."

"What if it's soup?" Hemingway asked from the corner, brushing off his jeans as he rose from the floor where he'd been working.

"You can drink it like a beverage," Paris said.

"You always have an answer." He chuckled.

"My point is that a ball gown makes the dance more alluring to those watching," Wilfred said, not at all amused. "Not only that, but the right gown not only complements the moves of a dancer, but it also encourages grace. When a woman wears a dress that flows with her moves, it becomes an extension of her."

The butler held out his white-gloved hand in a presenting fashion to the man beside him. "May I introduce an expert tailor, Juergen. His dresses are highly sought after and considered the finest quality. We are very fortunate that he is offering his skills to Happily Ever After College. He will be taking your measurements and designing and creating custom dresses for each of you."

There were several cheers of excitement around the room. They drowned out Paris' groan as she slumped. She held up her hand. "This is optional, right?"

Wilfred shook his head. "Absolutely not. All fairy godmothers must have a custom dress made for their final dance before graduation. Happily Ever After College holds a large ceremony for graduates and it's a requirement for passing."

The AI pointed at the trunk beside Juergen. "In there, you'll find swatches of materials, patterns for dresses, and various colors. While you wait to have your measurements taken, please look through your options. By the end of class today, I'd like you to have picked out the style of dress, color, and material. Please line up and let's get started on the next phase of your ballroom dancing curriculum."

Many of the students rushed forward, jockeying to get in line first or dive into the now open chest, pulling various materials from it. Paris and Christine hung back, watching the chaos from the sidelines.

"Well, I lasted longer at Happily Ever After College than I expected." Paris looked at her friend.

"You're quitting?" Christine challenged with a laugh.

Paris nodded. "I can put up with a lot. I'll learn to dance, stomach reading romance novels, and bite my tongue when archaic notions regarding astrology get passed off as fact, but I draw the line at wearing a dress. That's my threshold."

Hemingway chuckled, striding over and having heard Paris' comment. "You can't bring yourself to wear a dress? It seems like such a simple thing."

She lowered her chin and regarded him with hooded eyes. "Then why don't you wear one."

He laughed.

"Yeah, you'll look cute in a bright pink number," Christine joked.

Hemingway batted his eyes. "I thought turquoise in chiffon would match my eyes better."

"I picked turquoise for my ballroom dancing gown because it looks best with my orange hair," Christine explained.

"Oh, you've already done this then?" Paris asked.

"Yeah, you pick your dress in your first year, and Juergen delivers it right before graduation," Christine answered. "Poor guy is going to have to let my dress out some. I've put on weight since then, thanks to Chef Ash's cooking and desserts. Does that man put crack in his brownies? I must know."

"Knowing him, probably." Hemingway looked at Paris. "The graduation ball is really nice. I know you prefer leather jackets and combat boots, but it's nice to see all the fairy godmothers with their actual hair color and wearing their unique dresses made for them. It's quite the celebration."

"And it's a requirement?" Paris questioned.

"Yeah, you'll do a final dance that Wilfred grades," Christine replied. "Students are expected to show many of the skills we learned over the years. You know, etiquette, poise, manners, dancing, formalities, and charm."

"Question." Paris looked around, watching as fairies fought over large binders full of cloth swatches and patterns. "Where do they keep the barf bags during this event?"

Hemingway chuckled. "Maybe you can have one sewn into your dress."

Paris shook her head. "I'm not wearing a dress."

"You have to," Christine argued.

"Fine, but it's going to be made out of leather, and there will be pockets," Paris stated.

"And a place to keep your weapons, right?" Hemingway laughed.

"I hate to say this—"

"Then don't," Paris interrupted Christine. "I never understood why people prefaced things with that. If you don't want to say something, then simplify your life and don't. Anyone up for invading the kitchen for snacks? I'm hungry."

Her friend shook her head. "As I was saying, I think you're going to have to adapt in this situation. I know many things at the college challenge you, but that's part of growth. Wearing a dress isn't going to kill you."

Paris grimaced. "It might. I haven't tried. My demon blood might not allow it."

"Actually, it makes sense that you prefer such an edgy look," Hemingway observed. "I mean, your demon blood is a part of you."

"Blood usually is," Paris teased.

He grinned. "My point is that it would influence your style and a lot of things. I think Christine is right, though. Wearing a dress shouldn't be a deal-breaker for you. You've already rejected the uniform blue gown and gotten away with it. Maybe this is where you compromise and show that you're willing to adapt, sacrificing some of your preferences to observe the fairy godmother traditions."

Paris sighed, knowing that her friends were right. "Yeah, I guess you two Laffy Taffys are right." She tugged on Christine's arm, urging her forward. "Help me pick out stuff."

"You got it, girl," Christine sang proudly. "I think a sapphire blue would complement your eyes."

"I'm more concerned with finding something that complements my bad attitude," Paris countered.

"Try sequins then," Hemingway called at their backs. "Everyone will be distracted by the dazzle and not notice you frowning in your dress."

CHAPTER SEVEN

"A rare and powerful phenomenon is preparing to take place in the heavens," Professor Joyce Beacon said from the stage of the auditorium in the observatory.

Paris sat forward in her seat at the front of the classroom. If the mystic teacher wanted her attention, she had it. Picking out the color, materials, and style of the ballroom gown hadn't been as excruciating as Paris thought it would be, but that was probably because she let Christine make most of her decisions for her. Now she was grateful to be sitting in astrology class, even if most of the lessons were a bunch of hippie bullshit.

"Science would have you believe that the eight planets in our solar system only align every five hundred years," the professor continued in her airy tone.

Paris rolled her eyes. This was where the fairy godmother with the long grayish-blue dreadlocks always lost her. As soon as Professor Beacon started spouting stuff about astrology and saying that science didn't back it, Paris tuned her out.

She tried to remain open-minded but stating that there were no facts to support claims was one way to lose Paris' attention. She understood that many things in magic couldn't be fully understood, but it didn't mean that something real didn't back them up. However, saying that their zodiac predisposed people to be one way or another or that planetary retrogrades disrupted communications seemed ridiculous.

"The truth is that exact planetary alignment," Professor Beacon went on, "does happen only every five hundred years. Although the eight planets don't create a perfect line during other times of positioning, it still happens more frequently than some might know. And the magic that can be done during this brief moment of alignment and only during this time is rather extraordinary. For our lesson and a better understanding of this phenomenon, a visual is in order."

Professor Beacon removed a long dragonfly brooch attached to the shoulder of her blue gown and held it in the air. Paris guessed it was her magical instrument meant to channel her magic. A moment later, eight orbs of various sizes and colors appeared in the air over the students' heads, hovering. Paris recognized them as the planets in the solar system. They started to rotate and gradually move in different positions as a large yellow ball also appeared on the far side of them—the sun.

"On May 6, 2492, the planets will line up like this." Professor Beacon flicked her magical instrument softly, and the orbs all moved into a position unlike Paris had ever seen before where they were in a straight line. "However, in a few days, we will see an alignment, although not as orderly as this one," the fairy godmother continued, waving the brooch in the air. The eight plants all moved overhead, making more of a zigzag design.

Professor Beacon stood with her chin in the air and smiled. "You see, it's not a true alignment, but it's definitely more so than during normal times." When she returned her attention to the class, her wide eyes were alight with excitement. "The gravitational fields of the planets together create a massive effect on Earth. You see, notice that the planets partially obscure each other when aligned like this."

Paris lifted her chin, seeing what the professor was talking about but not putting together how this could create something powerful.

She was ready to tune out and not buy any of this science-ignoring mumbo-jumbo when Joyce Beacon summoned eight objects.

Little round mirrors rose to take positions between the planets rotating in the air. They all lined up beside each of the orbs, tilting until they each caught a beam of light and reflected it at a planet. The effect made a strange back and forth zig-zag like a kid's connect the dots.

"You see when the planets align like this, and someone uses mirror magic," Professor Beacon explained, "an interesting thing happens. Someone who knows what they're doing can hide something in plain sight for up to a few hours to possibly an entire day."

This revelation brought a series of excited whispers from the students. Professor Joyce, obviously looking for this reaction, smiled with satisfaction. "Many of the most perplexing robberies have happened during one of these alignments. Although criminals, these thieves knew to put mirrors into place in the area they intended to rob, to hide themselves and what they were stealing. It's quite fascinating."

"So this is used by criminal masterminds?" Paris was perplexed by this new information and not sure why. Although it wasn't entirely science-backed, she was still intrigued by it. Something about this information tugged at her core.

Professor Beacon nodded. "Most want to do what is right and have no reason to be invisible or hide something, so throughout history, these alignments have been used by those trying to break the law. The Loomis Fargo robbery where thieves stole seventeen million dollars from a bank vault was one of these robberies. The famous escape from Alcatraz of 1962 also happened during an alignment. And of course, the great robbery of Fort Knox."

"Wait," Paris argued. "Fort Knox has never been robbed."

The fairy godmother offered a sympathetic look. "That's what the authorities would have you believe. The moment someone learns that someone successfully robbed the seemingly impenetrable fortress, well, more will attempt it. I guess, more interesting than that someone was able to rob the place of tons of gold was that the authorities were able to cover it up so effectively."

"All of these things happened during one of the planetary alignments?" Penny Pullman asked from the back of the class. "Are there other noncriminal uses for this phenomenon?"

Professor Beacon tipped her head back and forth. "I've heard of practical reasons, like moving houses. Creating surprises. Doing reconnaissance. However, those usually aren't spoken about. It's the heists that have been mostly documented and therefore we know the most about."

"When is the next alignment?" Paris' heart suddenly beat fast, although she didn't know why.

"Four days," Professor Beacon answered.

Paris gulped, unsure why this information was so unsettling. However, she trusted her instinct, and right then it told her that this information on planetary alignment, mirrors, and hiding objects and people was important. She didn't know how it could come into play, but she was definitely going to pay closer attention to this, even if science didn't entirely support it.

CHAPTER EIGHT

"Today is a special day," Chef Ash began.

"It's a weird day," Paris muttered to herself from her workstation in the test kitchen classroom. Already she'd been fitted for and designed a dress and accepted a phenomenon not entirely backed by science. What next, she wondered. Was she going to make a steak dinner for a vegan? That would be on par with the rest of her day.

"Today, you are going to start working on your final project for the year," Chef Ash said proudly, pulling his pencil from behind his ear and flashing them all a grin. "By the end of this term, not only must you pass all of your exams to move on to the next level of fairy godmother studies, but to pass this class, you must present your signature dish."

That brought enthusiastic chatter from many in the classroom.

Holding up the pencil to gain everyone's attention, Chef Ash said, "Everyone needs a signature dish, whether you are a fairy, a fairy godmother, a magician, a mortal, a business person, a caregiver, or any other type of person holding any other position. Regardless of who you are, you must have a signature dish—something only you can make that knocks the socks off people."

Paris blinked at Chef Ash in confusion. "But why?"

He grinned, his eyes sparkling. "Because it makes people happy. It's your way to impress them. We all need something like that in our arsenal."

"Is this a dessert?" a student asked.

"It could be," Chef Ash answered. "It can be whatever you make that's best. Now finding your signature dish usually takes time. There will be experimentation, research, and a lot of soul searching.

"The idea is that you have to find that which makes your soul sing because then you'll make it with ease and your unique flair, and others will undoubtedly love it. If you find a dish you like to make that you're marginally good at, it's not your signature dish. This needs to be the one thing that you make better than everyone else in the world. And the only way to discover that is to look within."

Paris again was confused. "I'm sorry, I don't know how to soul-search a recipe. Do you have any concrete steps?"

"Sure. All of you answer this question personally. What's your favorite ingredient?" Chef Ash looked around the class.

There were answers from around the room:

"Chocolate."

"Bread."

"Pasta."

"Ice cream."

"Candy."

Paris didn't answer out loud, but she knew at once: cheese.

"Okay, so then consider what experience you most enjoy about that food," Chef Ash continued.

"Indulging," someone said.

"Filling up," another person stated.

"Feeling euphoric," a student offered.

Paris knew what she loved about a good cheese experience. It was snacking. Cheese made the best snack. It shouldn't be a meal on its own, but before or after dinner, it was perfect.

"Now that you know what you want to make and the experience you want it to offer, you start your research," Chef Ash explained. "Hopefully in time, you'll find the recipe that fits these two things.

Then you try to make it, and if you've gone in the right direction, you'll discover your signature dish. But if not, don't worry. This process is as much about the travels as it is about the destination, so try and enjoy exploring your options as you find the dish you'll use to wow people."

With that, Chef Ash clapped his hands, sending the students flurrying in all directions to comb through cookbooks or explore ingredients. Paris didn't know how cheese and the idea of snacking would lead to anything but a charcuterie board, although that was one of her favorite things.

She allowed this idea to lead her to a set of cookbooks. Before too long, a cornucopia of pictures of foods surrounded her. The images all seemed to stew together, making her think they were creating something new. Paris didn't know where it was leading her or what her signature dish might be, but it almost felt like she already had something in the oven, ready for the timer to go off and her to discover what it was that she'd made.

CHAPTER NINE

"There has to be a way you can help," Uncle John said, his face lined with worry when Paris entered the Fantastical Armory. She assumed since what was happening next was a momentous occasion that he'd be all smiles, but instead, he appeared upset. She guessed it was because of who he was speaking to.

"It's not my area of expertise," Subner grumbled, shaking his head of stringy, greasy black hair. His hands rested on a book in front of him on the glass countertop.

Exasperated, John glanced at Papa Creola, who was nearby, his long brown hair cleaner and hanging loosely around his long face. Father Time was wearing a tie-dye shirt that read, "I'd rather have flowers in my hair than diamonds around my neck."

Paris wanted to laugh at the image of flowers adorning the man's head.

"What about you?" Uncle John asked Papa Creola, his face pleading.

He shrugged in reply. "Not only is it not my expertise but it's not my interest. I dabble in time so why do I care what gets hidden during the planetary alignment?"

"Say what?" Paris asked, striding over, her ears perking up at the mention of the upcoming event she learned about in astrology class.

"Pare," Uncle John said, turning to face her, a smile breaking across his face. "I didn't expect you for a while longer."

She nodded. "I skipped out of my last class once I got the message from Papa Creola."

"A true sign of someone who will be a drain on society in the future," Subner mumbled. "Flaking out of your education handed to you even though you didn't qualify to get into the school. Real loser behavior."

Uncle John pursed his lips but didn't appear that put off by the insult. He was never as offended by the things people said as Paris was. His magic ability, if he had one, would be unyielding patience. "Pare was tested by the headmistress on her first week and earned her place at the school, although I know that her initial entry was a bit unorthodox."

"The arrangement was to keep her safe from the Deathly Shadow," Papa Creola stated matter-of-factly, then turned his attention to Paris. "Now it's your chosen field so taking it seriously is important, especially to Mama Jamba, who has a vested interest in you bringing love to the world."

Paris sighed. "Sorry, but when I get a message from you that I'm allowed to see my parents, who you guard, and also that my uncle finally gets to see them too, I'm skipping out of Magical Plants to get here."

Papa Creola rolled his eyes. "I'm not guarding them. Liv and Stefan have never and probably won't ever need guarding. I'm simply managing the process of how they assimilate into this timeline, and that involves slowly introducing them back to those they knew."

"I can't wait to see Liv...well, and Stefan too." Excitement bounced around in Uncle John's eyes. "I mean, I'm much closer to Liv, but your father is one of the best men I've had the pleasure of knowing. I wonder if they look different."

"Liv somehow managed to become more annoying," Subner related, as unhelpful and grumpy as ever.

Papa Creola shook his head. "They were gone a day. They look the same. They are the same. It's all of you who have changed."

"So when do they get to reenter the world?" Uncle John asked. "When does the House of Fourteen get to learn that they're back?"

Paris eyed her uncle, knowing that many things would affect everyone when her parents returned. For one, they would take their positions as Warriors for the House of Fourteen, which were protected for them by Fane and Alicia. However, when Alicia stepped down from that position, she could resume her old life—which was with Uncle John. The marriage to Uncle Clark was a sham, or it was originally, but it had been fifteen years. Maybe things had changed. Based on the look of uncertainty in Uncle John's eyes, that was his concern too.

"The timeline on that is still unclear," Papa Creola answered. "Liv and Stefan have been reintroduced to Paris and Plato. You, John, make the most sense to be the next person since you were there for Liv when her parents died and were a part of her transitioning."

"Not a coincidence, then, I'm guessing," Uncle John said with a sly smile. "I've thought for a long time that it wasn't chance that the young magician ended up knocking on my electronic repair shop and asking for a job the day she ran away from the House of Fourteen."

"You were a Mortal Seven," Papa Creola replied. "Although your powers and chimera were locked, it made sense for her to be around you to protect her magic until she decided to use it again."

When someone murdered Paris' grandparents, Liv ran away from the House of Fourteen, choosing to have her magic locked.

"I thought so," Uncle John said proudly.

Paris however wasn't as impressed by this admission. "Always orchestrating things in our lives, aren't you?" she asked Papa Creola, thinking of all the ways he'd set up things in her life, like her attending Happily Ever After College.

"Unfortunately, he's always orchestrating things that help you to stay alive," Subner complained. "Hopefully soon he'll sign off on arranging for a bus to cross your path at full speed."

Paris stuck her tongue out at the angry elf. "Too bad for you that I look both ways when I cross the street."

Subner sighed, disappointed. "I encourage you to have more faith in your longevity and do things blindly."

"Well, I'm glad I finally get to see those two," Uncle John said eagerly to Papa Creola, ignoring Paris and Subner's banter. "That's a start to things returning to normal."

"Yes, and hopefully your chimera will return soon," Paris said, thinking about Pickles, who had hidden in her locket and helped her with the Deathly Shadow.

Uncle John nodded. "Pickles is out there somewhere, watching over us as he does. I look forward to seeing him, but not more than Liv."

Papa Creola waved at the door at the back of the shop that led to the basement. "They're waiting for you. Go on down as soon as Paris asks her burning question."

Surprised, Uncle John glanced at Paris. "What burning question."

She blinked at Papa Creola. "If you know my burning question, why don't you answer it?"

"Because I don't feel like it."

Paris huffed and turned her attention to Uncle John. "When I entered the shop, you all were talking about the upcoming planetary alignment. What's going on? What's being hidden?"

"You've learned about planetary alignment then," Uncle John stated, nodding.

"Yeah, recently."

"I don't know who or what is trying to be hidden, but I'd like to stop it." Uncle John withdrew a small round mirror from his pocket and held it up. "I found this in the hallway of the jail at FLEA."

"A mirror." Paris gasped, reached out, and took the small object.

"Oh, good, you can identify simple things," Subner retorted and returned to reading his book or at least pretending to do so.

"I can also identify you as an annoyance who serves no real purpose." She studied the mirror. It appeared completely normal, although small for its size.

"Without me, there would be massive wars and total annihilation of the human race," Subner stated matter-of-factly.

Surprised, Paris shot a furtive look at Papa Creola, expecting him to dispute this piece of information.

Instead, the hippie elf nodded. "It's true. Subner is the Protector of Weapons and guards them against creating massive destruction."

"Well, is that why you're so grumpy?" Paris asked. "Because you have a difficult job, but you have a pure heart under all the bitter exterior."

"I'm irritable because my job inadvertently has me keeping people like you alive," Subner answered.

She batted her eyes at him. "And here I thought I should thank Papa Creola for keeping me safe."

"Unfortunately, it's a team effort," he admitted.

Paris held up the small mirror, looking at Uncle John. "Someone put this in the hallway of the jail area at FLEA?"

"I think so," he answered. "I only found that one, but there are probably more. That's what I hoped Subner or Papa Creola could help me with. I think I found this one because the wards used to hide it don't work on mortals, but whoever placed it there won't know that a mortal is regularly in the Fairy Law Enforcement Agency."

A part of Uncle John's secret identity, besides that he wasn't a fairy, was that he was a mortal on Roya Lane—the only one allowed to enter thanks to his magitech wings.

"So you think there are more? Why?" Paris laid the mirror on the glass countertop.

"Well, you know how hiding objects or people during a planetary alignment works," Uncle John stated. "To set it up, mirrors have to be placed into various positions before the event."

"Yes, it has something to do with the refraction of light during the alignment that hides things." Paris had researched the subject after astrology class, fascinated by the concept, which required setup, a fair bit of magic, and timing. "Then you think that someone is planning to do something in the jail in four days?"

Uncle John stuck his hands in his trouser pants and shrugged. "I'm not certain. It makes the most sense, but I haven't found any other mirrors yet. I think some might have other spells on them that work on me. To stop whoever is behind this, I'd need to find all of the mirrors and remove them."

"Who would want to enter the FLEA jail?" Paris scratched her head.

"Hard to say," Uncle John answered. "There are hundreds of criminals that are housed there on any given day as well as evidence lockers, top-secret files, and who knows what else could be of value to a criminal."

"You can't help?" Paris asked Papa Creola.

"Won't," Father Time answered simply. "It's not my jurisdiction to meddle in such things."

"But it's about justice," Paris argued, her anger suddenly flaring. "If someone is planning to do something at the FLEA jail and you know something and can help, why don't you?"

Papa Creola gathered his shoulder-length hair in his hand and wrapped it into a knot on the top of his head, pinning it in place as if it had suddenly started to annoy him. "It doesn't work that way. Just because I know things and can intervene doesn't mean I should. The gods of this world were all given specific jobs for a reason. If I interfered in things that didn't pertain to time, I could cause problems for others.

"We can't all do all things. That's why we divided up the responsibility. FLEA is John's jurisdiction. Planetary alignment is part of Mama Jamba's organizational plans. Hidden objects belong to the centaurs. None of that pertains to me, so I'm staying out of it."

Quelling her frustration at Papa Creola, Paris offered Uncle John a hopeful look. "Maybe Mama Jamba will help. Or the centaurs who know a lot about astrology can offer insights."

Subner laughed coldly. "The centaurs are about as likely to help as I am to give you a back rub."

She grimaced at the thought of having the greasy elf's hands on her. "What about Mother Nature? She maybe can help."

"She's busy fixing a vortex that some brainless dimwit opened to a parallel dimension," Subner stated dryly.

Paris shook her head at him. "I was rescuing my parents under Papa Creola's direction."

"He's right," Papa Creola offered. "Although it was necessary to open the vortex to the other dimension, doing so created a few problems on this planet. We knew it would, and Mama Jamba was ready to start her work as soon as it opened, but fixing things before they spill over into the waking world and cause natural disaster has taken her out for a while."

"Not to mention that a problem at FLEA is beneath Mother Nature's paygrade," Subner said, his attention still on his book, although he hadn't turned the page.

Paris' frustration built knowing that the gods of that world so often didn't care to help or "interfere" as Papa Creola put it. "Uncle John, can I help look for the mirrors?"

"I really don't want you in the jail area, Pare."

She sighed, drumming her fingers on her lips. "Well, then keep an eye out for them. And maybe you can consult the guest list when you find them and correlate it to who could be placing them."

"That's a good idea," Uncle John stated. "It makes the most sense that someone is trying to break someone out of jail, which means we need to up our security on our prisoners. I'll work on something covert that traps them in the jail during the time of the planetary alignment."

"That's a good idea," Paris affirmed. "That way, if someone is successful at getting into the jail or hiding a prisoner so they can get out, they still won't be able to leave the Fairy Law Enforcement Agency."

"That's what I'm thinking," Uncle John said proudly. "It will give whoever is behind this false confidence because when they stroll out of their jail, they'll think they are free, but they won't expect a trap at the entrance. It will be a perfect place to reveal our culprit."

Paris smiled, impressed by how strategic her uncle was. "Well, let me know how I can help."

"You can get out of here, so I can read without being interrupted by your incessant yammering," Subner quipped, hammering on his open book. "Otherwise, I might be tempted to start some wars rather than keep them from demolishing Earth."

Uncle John smiled good-naturedly, put his arm around Paris' shoulder, and steered her toward the door at the back of the shop. "We'll get out of your hair. Enjoy your book."

Paris shivered. "Great, now I have to shower, thinking of the idea of being in Subner's greasy hair." She offered the grumpy elf a rude glare before turning back around and heading through the door, singing over her shoulder. "I read that book you have. He dies."

Subner slammed the book shut, groaning.

Paris laughed. "Yammer, yammer, yammer."

CHAPTER TEN

Paris got a sudden reminder of Uncle John's age and the fact that he was a mortal as they descended the hundreds of stairs to the basement where her parents were staying in Papa Creola's personal space.

Uncle John had to stop a few times to rest, his breathing heavy. Seeing the look on her face, he managed a pained smile and held up his hand. "I'm fine, Pare."

"You're wheezing," she countered.

"I'm not at my strongest if Pickles isn't with me," he explained. "When you lived with me and had the locket, it kept me from aging as rapidly."

"But because Pickles isn't around, you're not as strong?" she asked, suddenly worried and conscious of how much weaker her Uncle John was. He was and had never been a fairy who had long lives of up to a thousand years.

He chuckled. "Without Pickles in proximity, I'm a normal mortal once more."

Paris didn't find this at all funny. "Then we have to reunite you with Pickles."

"We will," he said calmly, still catching his breath. "When the time is right. I went most of my life with that chimera locked away. Another stint isn't going to kill me."

She grimaced. "Bad choice of words."

Uncle John waved her off. "Oh, don't you worry. What did I tell you when you were little and used to stress over things?"

Paris didn't have to think about the question. Automatically she said, "Leave worrying to me. You be a kid, and I'll be the adult."

He nodded. "Exactly."

"But I am an adult now," Paris argued.

Uncle John smiled fondly at her. "I know, but you'll always be my little Pare. Now let's go see your parents and not think on this one moment longer."

Paris knew that arguing would only cause more stress for Uncle John, which would make things worse. She reluctantly agreed, having more motivation than before to get her parents out of this basement and into the real world. Before, she wanted everyone to know that they were back and life to feel normal. However, now she wanted John reunited with Pickles so that he was back to his old self—and by that, she meant younger, healthier self.

CHAPTER ELEVEN

At the sight of John and Paris coming down the stairs, Liv peeled herself off the sofa overlooking the seemingly real view of West Hollywood. Her blonde hair swept back as she rushed in a blur toward Uncle John. However, Liv stopped short of embracing him.

Her brow knit together, and she tilted her head, studying Uncle John. "You look different."

Uncle John's arms were wide, and he kept them extended as he chuckled. "You look the same. Now come here."

Liv fell easily into Uncle John's arms, hugging him tightly, her eyes connecting with Paris over his shoulder, smiling at her fondly. Uncle John squeezed her tightly and to Liv's and Paris' surprise, he hauled her off her feet, swinging her back and forth with obvious delight.

"I've missed you so very much!" Uncle John set Liv back on her feet.

She peeled away while shaking her head at him. "You're going to throw out your back if you attempt that again."

He shook his head. "No, I won't. I'm as fit as I was fifteen years ago."

Stefan had hung back for the reunion. Now he strode over,

offering an extended hand. "So good to see you, John. How have you been?"

John eagerly wrung his hand, smiling wide as Liv took the opportunity to hug her daughter.

"I've been good," Uncle John stated. "I'm sure Pare has filled you in on all the details. My life is different than you all remember it."

"You've aged." Liv crossed her arms over her chest in a challenging manner as Stefan hugged Paris. She didn't think she'd ever get used to having her parents around. She hoped that she did, although she'd never take them for granted.

Uncle John chuckled again. "Again, you were gone fifteen years. We all aged." He indicated Paris beside him. "Remember when she was a tiny little thing?"

"Still is." Stefan looked his daughter over.

Liv combed her fingers through her hair. "It's so strange. It feels like you were younger a week ago, John. I can't imagine how weird it will be when I see the others."

"I guess I understand why Papa Creola isn't allowing everyone here at once," Stefan stated. "It's a lot to process."

"Soph pretty much looks the same thanks to the chi of the dragon," Uncle John explained. "Clark too, thanks to his disciplined lifestyle. King Ru hasn't aged a bit. Rory has some grays, but he says you gave those to him before you disappeared, Liv."

Liv laughed. "That's totally true. Also, giants and gnomes don't age so gracefully, much like mortals." She sized John up again with a scrutinizing expression. "Have you been taking your heart meds still, old man?"

He shook his head. "You know that with Pickles around, I don't need that stuff. But regardless of the magic of the chimera, I'm going to age, Liv. It's inevitable."

"Not to mention that I've put years on his life with my antics," Paris related, hoping to make light of the seriousness of the moment, reading the worry on her mother's face.

Uncle John shook his head. "Oh, no, you didn't, Pare. You kept me young. FLEA might have caused me a few wrinkles though."

"Not to mention uprooting your whole life, John," Stefan said, his face suddenly serious. "Actually, this is a good time to thank you for everything. Most importantly, thanks for taking care of our daughter. I know you had to give up everything to do it and you did an incredible job."

All three of them gazed at Paris fondly, suddenly making her nervous—her ears grew hot.

"Raising Pare was the biggest honor of my entire life," Uncle John said fondly. "The others gave up things: Seeing Paris grow up, being restricted from Roya Lane, having to take positions or marry to cover your positions in the House of Fourteen. Not one person minded, but I'm the only one who gave up nothing and got the privilege of watching your amazing daughter grow up. Thank you…"

Liv elbowed her husband. "See, I told you. He hasn't changed a bit. John gives up the electronic repair shop, his relationship with Alicia, and takes on a detective job as a fairy, and he turns around and thanks us." She shook her head, smiling fondly. "You really are the best of the best, aren't you, John."

"Not at all," he replied shyly. "But I sure did miss you and your belief in me, Liv."

The two had a silent moment as they regarded each other. Stefan put his arm around Paris and led her over to the sitting room, giving Liv and John a private moment. The place looked as it had before, apparently magicked to look like the apartment where they lived over the electronic repair shop.

"How are you?" He gestured for her to sit.

Paris slid onto the white sofa, her black pants and leather jacket contrasting starkly with it. "I'm good," Then she updated him on all the things that had been going on at the college like Faraday, murders, and more. It felt better than she ever could have imagined having her parents to share her experiences with. They were such attentive listeners.

"Do you think it's an open-and-shut case with Agent Topaz?" Liv asked Uncle John. The pair had joined the others on the couch.

He thought for a moment. "Pare has her instincts on this, and I'm keeping an eye out for evidence to support her suspicions, but currently, it looks like Topaz will end up convicted of murder. The case against him is pretty solid. He's not doing himself any favors by not answering our questions. We've been trying to figure out how he made the poison, and all he keeps saying is that he doesn't know. The guy's a mess and full of stutters—"

"As if maybe he can't talk," Paris interrupted as the realization dawned on her.

Uncle John pursed his lips and looked skeptical. "I don't know, Pare. Usually, criminals don't want to because they'll further indict themselves."

"What if Agent Topaz has been spelled, like when Papa Creola spelled you all not to be able to tell me anything about my parents," Paris offered.

Liv and Stefan glanced back and forth, following the conversation.

"Well, if that's the case when Topaz gives his testimony, it will break the spell," Uncle John explained. "We don't have the magic to take such wards down during investigations since they interfere with our security measures in the jail. However, in FLEA court, those kinds of silencing spells don't work, and if Topaz has something to say that speaks to his innocence, it will come out. That's how justice works, anyway. The trial will prove him innocent or guilty."

Liv looked up longingly. "I can't wait to get back to the world and deliver justice once more. This conversation makes me hungrier for it."

"I wish your boss wasn't against protecting justice." Paris explained how Papa Creola refused to help them with whatever someone was orchestrating in the FLEA jail during the planetary alignment.

"That's odd," Stefan replied when finished.

"Not the part about Papa not helping," Liv stated. "That man has made it quite clear to me on multiple occasions that the only injustices he stands against are the ones that violate time. The gods of this world are excellent at turning a blind eye when something falls on the other side of the jurisdiction."

"Yeah, I remember how infuriating that was, knowing they could help but don't," Stefan related.

"Do either of you have any experience with such things?" Uncle John leaned forward, his elbows pinned on his knees.

Liv glanced at her husband with a pensive expression. Finally, she shook her head. "I think you're right, John. You can see the mirrors because a ward that doesn't work on mortals is operating. However, if I were a mastermind planning an escape at a jail, I'd have multiple things in place just in case. Mirrors hidden by magic. Others hidden from mortals. Also, ones that were just plain hidden. Then an expert cleaning crew couldn't foil my plans."

"That's one thing that always made your mother good as a Warrior," Stefan said to Paris, indicating Liv. "She's good at thinking like a villain."

"Although I'm not one," Liv cut in defensively.

"Wait, cleaning crew!" Uncle John exclaimed suddenly, nearly making Paris jump.

Liv's eyes widened, and she jumped to her feet. "Of course, John. That's a genius idea."

"Can you get me in there?" Uncle John asked.

Both Paris and Stefan wore confused expressions, not having followed the two.

"No, since I'm not up on Roya Lane," Liv said, deflating before perking up. "However, my offspring would be allowed in the office."

John's and Liv's gazes shifted to Paris. She blushed, wondering what they were talking about.

"What office?" Paris asked nervously.

"The Official Brownie Headquarters," Liv answered. "John won't be able to get in there because you need a personal invite and he's a mortal. However, I always had a standing invite to the office on Roya Lane. Sophia does too because their leader often helped us with cases."

"You mean those little elves who supposedly clean houses at night," Paris guessed.

"Not supposedly," Liv stated. "They do."

"So Brownies helped you with cases?" Paris found that strange.

"Who better than the little elves who have eyes and floppy ears everywhere," Stefan agreed, apparently privy to the covert sources Liv used.

"Mortimer was…well, is a good friend of mine," Liv stated. "He should still be the leader. I can tell you where to find their office on Roya Lane."

Paris blinked, picturing Roya Lane, which she knew incredibly well. "There's not a Brownie office up above."

"Not that most see," Liv corrected. "Like I said, you have to be invited. I'm guessing that if you go to the place I tell you, knock on the wall, and state who you are, you'll be granted entry. They'll know you're my daughter and that the only way you knew where to find them was because I told you."

"So you want me to go to the Official Brownie Headquarters, and then what?" Paris hadn't followed her uncle's and mother's sudden realization that excited them both.

"Brownies are excellent at cleaning up stuff," Uncle John stated.

Paris nodded. "I followed as much."

"Things hidden by magic or other means," Liv continued.

"Oh!" Paris exclaimed. "So you think that the Brownies, if I ask them, will clean up the mirrors in the jail, preventing whatever was going to happen during the planetary alignment from happening?"

"I do," Liv stated.

"And to be on the safe side," Uncle John added, "I'll put in extra security measures on the day of the alignment that prevents anyone from leaving by the exit."

"Good idea," Stefan stated. "That will be easier to guard with magic than if you put individual security wards on each of the cells. One block instead of multiple locks."

"Uncle John is the smartest." Paris looked at him fondly.

Liv twirled her finger, conjuring a piece of paper and a pen. Papa Creola had refused to allow her to have a phone yet, saying that the updates to technology would mess with her ability to assimilate into the current time smoothly. "I'll draw you a map of where to find the Official Brownie Headquarters."

"In the meantime," Stefan smiled, "tell us more about what's been going on at the college."

Paris sat back and frowned. "Well, sadly, it looks like I'm unable to get out of wearing a ball gown for one of my graduation requirements." Something occurred to her suddenly. "Hey, is it my demon blood that makes it so I don't like wearing frilly dresses and prefer black?"

Liv laughed, looking up from the drawing she was sketching. "Oh, no. You inherited that from your parents. Stefan and I have always been monochromatic in our color choices."

Paris' father nodded. "Yeah, try sneaking up on an evil villain while wearing a bright neon vest. It's impractical."

"But for various cases," Liv continued, "even I have been forced to wear a dress. It's important to remember that wearing high heels is as necessary as executing a roundhouse kick. The only things outside your wheelhouse are the things your ego dictates."

Uncle John smiled at Paris. "I know you'll wear that dress with grace, and I can't wait to see it at your graduation ceremony."

Her parents both shared the affectionate expression on Uncle John's face. Stefan nodded proudly. "Us too. We will definitely be there."

CHAPTER TWELVE

"Oh for the love of the gods," Christine gushed, throwing her head back. "That's the best thing I've ever tasted."

Chef Ash heard the exclamation and hurried over, a curious expression on his face. He glanced down at the round object on the worktops sitting on a plate between Paris and Christine and looked up, confused. The mound of cheese covered in crushed nuts and parsley sort of looked like a brain, which wasn't the most appetizing thing…well, unless one was a zombie. Then it was probably decadent in appearance.

"Your signature dish is a cheese ball?" he asked Paris with uncertainty.

She scrunched up her nose and smiled. "Is that okay? I know it doesn't require much work or cooking or baking, but it's—"

"The best thing I've ever tasted," Christine cut in, taking another cracker and combing it down the side of the cheeseball, messing up its shape but not caring.

Chef Ash picked up a cracker and held it next to the side of the cheeseball, pausing for a moment. "The thing is, a signature dish or any other one doesn't have to be complex. That's not part of the keys I described to you. It has to include an ingredient you enjoy and an experience you crave. Does your cheeseball do that?"

"Well, yeah," Paris stated. "I love cheese, and I love snacking."

"That's why I love this halfling," Christine gushed, taking another cracker and cutting around Chef Ash to get a proper bite, relishing the taste.

"Then you've done what I asked, and it has to deliver at this point," Chef Ash continued, sliding his cracker down the side of the cheeseball and covering it with soft cream cheese and spices. "The thing is, the most satisfying signature dishes don't have to be complicated. They have to be true to the person who made them. And I dare say, most of us are very simple beings. People stumble, unable to find their true signature dish when they don't know themselves, thinking they're rather complex when they aren't or the other way around."

He lifted the bite to his mouth, pausing and giving Paris a challenging look that made her hold out her hands to stop him from eating.

"Maybe this isn't it though," she argued. "I'm a halfling with demon blood studying the thing I loathe most—romance. Maybe I picked the wrong dish and need to try something else before you taste."

"Or maybe the most complex of us prefers the simplest things," he stated and popped the cracker covered in cheeseball into his mouth, his face transforming at once.

His expression went from curious to pleasant to surprise in a matter of seconds. "That's perfect."

"W-Wh-What?" Paris was sure he had misspoken.

"I told you." Christine took another cracker. "It's so good that it's wrong. I'm now calling you Cheeseball."

"Fair enough, Christina," Paris teased.

"You see why I have to resort to name-calling?" Christine asked.

Chef Ash pointed at the mound of cheese. "That's good. Like, it's really good. What all did you do...no, don't give up your secrets."

Paris looked around. "So do you think this is my signature dish?"

"Without a doubt." Chef Ash grabbed another cracker and nudged Christine over to get access to the delectable treat.

"Others have found their dishes too, right?" Paris asked.

"I only know mine must include cilantro," Christine stated. "I love too much cilantro. It's my thing."

Chef Ash shook his head. "Usually it takes a fairy godmother their entire time here at Happily Ever After College to nail down their signature dish."

"Oh, then I haven't found it yet," Paris said, her eyes wide as she stared down at her mostly demolished cheeseball. "I'll keep researching."

Chef Ash offered her a caring look. "Sometimes we arrive at our destination earlier than others but have a hard time being there or need time to figure out how to set up camp. Sometimes it takes us a while to find our destination, and we instantly know it. Don't worry. You're not going to achieve at the same rate as others here. We would never expect that. You have indeed found your signature dish, but maybe over time, you'll figure out how to improve upon it or really put your mark on it. The good news is that you have time to figure it out."

Christine pulled the cheeseball toward her as if it was all hers at this point. "If there's improving upon this, give me the marriage license because Mr. Cheeseball and I are getting hitched."

Chef Ash shook his head at her. "I don't need to tell you how wrong it is to marry a plate of food, right?"

"You might," Christine said in between bites.

The three laughed, Paris letting out a relieved sigh that she'd had such a nice victory. She only wished that wearing the ball gown would come so easily for her.

CHAPTER THIRTEEN

The greenhouse was filled with cut flowers and greenery when Paris entered, making it look more like a florist shop. Hemingway was wearing a cunning grin when she took her seat at her usual station.

"Plants, especially magical ones, have many different uses," Hemingway began when the class had quieted, giving him their attention. "As we've learned, there are medicinal purposes as well as practical ones and everything in between. Today, we're going to learn how plants can serve as a visual attraction. I'll be teaching you about a very important art form."

Paris was instantly intrigued and leaned forward in her seat, wondering what this art form could be.

Hemingway swept his hand at the mass of cut flowers on the table in the center of the greenhouse. "Today, you'll learn the art of flower arranging."

As quickly as she got excited, Paris deflated at once with a sigh. She had thought the lesson would be interesting and useful, but it sounded like it would be as helpful as learning how to ballroom dance.

Hemingway's gaze caught her look of disappointment, but he

didn't appear deterred by her expression. "Alice Walker, a novelist, wrote that 'In nature, nothing is perfect and everything is perfect.' The idea with flower arrangements is to take what nature has already made perfect and put it together in a way that capitalizes on its beauty."

Paris wished she could have skipped this lesson to work on something more worth her time and efforts.

"I bet some of you," Hemingway continued, giving Paris a very pointed expression, "think that flower arrangement is as simple as throwing some stuff into a vase."

Paris nodded. "Just because the result looks pretty, I don't think we can call it an art form."

He grinned, again not appearing put off by her always rebellious attitude. "Yes, but I would contend one can toss some flowers in a mason jar, and it looks nice, but someone who knows the fundamentals of arranging can make it appear outstanding."

Hemingway strode forward and picked up a fiddlehead fern still curled in on itself. "One of the keys to unique flower arrangement is to pick things to go in your centerpiece that are unexpected and interesting. Things like branches of berries, nuts, or grapevines are all nice and add a different texture than soft flowers."

Paris stifled a yawn, thinking that maybe she could sneak out of the class in a bit and go to the Official Brownie Headquarters. She was intrigued by the notion of meeting a Brownie, the house elves that were quite elusive and not seen by most.

"Another important fundamental to flower arranging," Hemingway continued, picking up a long-stemmed rose, "is to have things of various heights in your bouquet. The idea is to create something that isn't only visually pleasing to look at but inspiring, comforting, appetizing, or many other things. The key is to think of where this arrangement will sit, what feelings and thoughts you want it to inspire, and allow the things you've picked from nature to tell you how they should work together."

Oh good. That doesn't seem like a hippie thing to do: Have your flowers talk to you.

She was a bit surprised that Hemingway of all people was teaching such a lesson. The magician in disguise as a fairy tended to be very practical with his curriculum. The art of flower arranging seemed like something that one of the more emotional and hippie-ish professors would be teaching.

"You'll find various books about flower arranging on the back shelf," Hemingway stated, waving to the far corner of the greenhouse. "Your project today is to create a centerpiece that is both attractive to look at as well as unique. That means you'll have to think outside the vase, if you will." He winked, making many of the girls blush and giggle.

Having been set loose, many of the students jumped to their feet, hurrying for the cut flowers and books. Paris ducked, thinking that she could use the distraction of the moment to sneak out of the greenhouse.

Surely helping Uncle John figure out what was going on at the FLEA jail was more important than putting some peonies into a vase and calling it art.

Paris slid through the students bustling in the opposite direction and made her way to the exit on the other side of the greenhouse. She was almost to the door when Hemingway cut her off, appearing seemingly out of nowhere—his arms crossed over his chest and a challenging grin on his face.

"Where do you think you're going, Miss Beaufont?"

CHAPTER FOURTEEN

The truth seemed like the best thing to disclose at that point so Paris launched straight into it in a murmur, not wanting anyone else to overhear.

"That does sound like a good reason to skip out of my class," Hemingway offered when Paris had finished telling him about the strange events going on at the FLEA jail and how she needed to recruit the Brownies' help.

"I thought you'd think so." Paris eyed the door.

"The thing is," Hemingway continued, still blocking her way to the exit. "The planetary alignment isn't for a few days."

"Yeah, but we need to prepare for whatever is going to happen," Paris argued.

"I don't disagree," Hemingway stated. "I also need to prepare for something and hoped that you could help me. It needs to happen before the planetary alignment because the energy field it creates could complicate things so it takes precedence on your side quest to bring justice—yet again."

"You need my help?" Paris pointed at herself in surprise. "With what?"

He leaned forward, bowing his head. "Something you said stuck with me."

She blinked at him again, astonished. "What?"

"Well, pretty much everything you say," he replied with a laugh. "But I think it's time I let someone go. It feels like it's time and what is keeping me stuck."

Once more, Paris was shocked. "You mean…"

She let the sentence trail off unfinished, not wanting to fill in the details in case someone was listening.

He nodded, understanding her thoughts. They both knew who he was referring to—the ghost of Hemingway's mother who haunted the Bewilder Forest.

It made sense that clearing the ghost needed to happen before the planetary alignment, which had assorted effects on magic. They might have to wait a long time if they did it afterward, once the energy reset. Paris was confused about what Hemingway needed her for though. She didn't know anything about ghosts or getting rid of them.

"What do you want my help with?" she whispered.

"Well, it has to do with today's lesson," he answered.

"Oh," she said, disappointed.

"You see, I think that creating a shrine of sorts would be nice," he continued.

"That makes sense." She thought it would be symbolic, like flowers at a grave, helping Hemingway to let go.

"As I told the class, flower arranging is about finding something unique for the display," Hemingway stated. "That's where you come in. I can't find the right thing here at Happily Ever After College. I thought maybe there was a shop on Roya Lane that had something—a rare flower or a plant with unique properties. Since you know that place better than anyone else, I hoped you could take me."

Paris smiled. "I'd be honored. While I'm there, maybe I can swing by the Brownie headquarters."

Hemingway nodded. "Exactly. It's a win-win. Now, aren't you glad you didn't sneak out of here before talking to me?"

She tucked her chin, trying to cover up her small bit of shame. "Yeah, sorry about that. But I'm grateful you want my help."

He held out his hand to the door, stepping to the side. "Well, since you didn't want to do today's assignment, I say we head out now."

She glanced over her shoulder where the other students were working. "What about the class?"

"They'll be fine." He winked. "A perk of being the professor is I get to leave class whenever I want and don't have to sneak."

CHAPTER FIFTEEN

Hemingway's face was covered in awe when they stepped through the portal to Roya Lane. It was interesting to Paris that before going to Happily Ever After College, she'd hardly ever been off the street full of magical shops and offices. Ironically, Hemingway had hardly ever left the bubble of fairy godmother college. She imagined that his fascination while looking around Roya Lane was similar to hers when she first stepped onto the Enchanted Grounds.

"I didn't know it was so small." Hemingway blinked at the various shops with colorful display windows.

"Don't be deceived." Paris pulled him to the side to make room for a pair of giants to pass. They hardly cared where they were going or if someone was in their way—mowing over magicians and fairies and rarely apologizing for it. "Roya Lane is full of all sorts of hidden places, alleyways I've yet to explore, and things I didn't know existed like the Official Brownie Headquarters. It seems compact, but I have a feeling it's much larger than anyone completely realizes."

"Very cool." Hemingway's gaze ran over the cobbled lane and the strange characters striding by them. Most didn't notice them, too preoccupied with their own business. "So, where do you think we should go to find a unique flower or plant for my mother's shrine?"

It was nice that they could talk more freely now that they weren't at the college. "Good question. Although I don't know all the shops here, I have connections and know people who do."

Paris made her way to the Crying Cat Bakery, thinking that Lee might be able to help. If not, she could pop into the Rose Apothecary and ask Bep, the potions expert. Then again, she could impress Hemingway and take him to the Fantastical Armory and introduce him to Papa Creola, although she wasn't in the mood for Subner's insults. Also, it might tempt her to pop down and see her parents.

Before Paris could make up her mind, the person who might help her decided things for her—and she couldn't have picked a worse advisor.

King Rudolf Sweetwater popped around a corner, a toothy grin on his face that quickly disappeared at the sight of Hemingway. "Oh, I must be straight up trippin' because my niece is in the presence of possibly the worst human being since Stefan Ludwig was born."

CHAPTER SIXTEEN

Hemingway didn't appear offended by the fae's comment. Instead, he seemed amused.

"This is your uncle?" Hemingway asked, looking King Rudolf over. He was wearing a plum purple tunic and silk pants. His wings were glamoured not to show, the same as Paris and Hemingway. His blond hair was perfectly in place, making him look as handsome as ever.

"Technically, he's my pseudo uncle because we're not related by blood," Paris explained, giving him an apologetic look.

"I'm Paris Beaufont's mother's best friend in all the world," King Rudolf explained proudly, holding a hand to his chest. "Although never formally named, everyone assumed that I was her godfather, so I'm more than an uncle."

Paris didn't think that was at all true, but she wasn't going to argue with him. "Hemingway, this is King Rudolf Sweetwater."

Hemingway appeared suddenly impressed, holding out a hand to Rudolf. "What an honor. Nice to meet you. You're the king of the fae?"

Rudolf stuck his nose in the air, not taking the offered hand. "I am, and I don't touch men's hands who look so rugged and dashing. Have you considered wearing a mask to cover up your face?"

Hemingway glanced at Paris. "I can't tell if he's insulting me or complimenting."

Paris nodded. "That's pretty typical of the king."

"I don't tolerate men who are handsome enough to rival my beautiful looks," King Rudolf stated, his chin still held high into the air.

"Well, thank you, I think." Hemingway drew out the last word with uncertainty.

"Maybe you can help us," Paris began. "We're looking for a shop on Roya Lane that specializes in rare and unique plants. I'm not aware of one, but I know that not all the places are known here."

"That's correct," the fae stated. "Some shops only appear on a full moon or during the summer solstice or in the past or if you're wearing Crocs…although those people really should be put in jail and not given special access to a shop."

"Right." Paris wasn't sure if she should believe King Rudolf or not. He was incredibly knowledgeable but also said the looniest things.

"You're looking for the Glowing Orchid," King Rudolf stated. "Entry is by invitation only, which I can help you with." He held out his hand, and a golden card magically appeared.

Paris took it, reading the embossed text. "King Rudolf Sweetwater grants permission to Guinevere Paris Beaufont and her homely friend to enter the Glowing Orchid."

"Thanks." Hemingway laughed.

"What I can't help you with is the trade you'll need if you wish to get any of the items in the shop," King Rudolf stated.

"Trade?" Paris asked.

"Yes, the owner, Astrid, doesn't take money for purchases," King Rudolf explained. "She only takes trade, and it will depend on what you want, what she's in the market for, and what she had for breakfast that day."

"Not weird at all." Hemingway was growing more amused by King Rudolf's antics.

"So we go to this shop and find out what this Astrid wants," Paris said, not at all deterred or surprised that this task would send them on a wild goose chase. "Where is the Glowing Orchid?"

"It's right between my store, Heals Pills, and the Rose Apothecary," the king answered.

Paris shook her head. "No, I've been by there a thousand times, and there's no shop between those two stores."

King Rudolf pointed at the card. "You've never had an invitation before. Hold the golden card as you approach, and the Glowing Orchid will appear."

"Much like the phrase, 'when the pupil is ready, the master will appear,'" Hemingway offered.

King Rudolf rolled his eyes. "You're smart and good-looking. You might be worse than Paris' father. I think it's better if when in my presence you don't speak. That will keep me from employing Lee's services."

"Lee's services?" Hemingway looked at Paris to clarify.

"She's a baker," Paris answered.

The confusion on Hemingway's face deepened. "Oh, I don't under-stand. If I'm not quiet when I'm around you, King Rudolf, you're going to buy me a cake?"

He shook his head. "No, her other services."

Hemingway looked sideways at Paris.

"She's also an assassin," she explained.

"Oh, got it." Hemingway pretended to zip his mouth and throw away the imaginary key.

"Good man," King Rudolf cheered. "You might not be as awful as Stefan Ludwig after all." He then bowed to Paris, offering her a proud smile. "Until we meet again, my darling niece. I will be counting the seconds until I'm graced with your presence and can offer you my invaluable wisdom once more."

"Yeah, I can't wait." Paris held up the gold card. "Thank you for the invitation."

King Rudolf sighed. "You're welcome. Unfortunately, thanks to a promise I made to your mother, I can't require one hundred years of servitude from a Beaufont in exchange for favors. It is the custom of the fae to have invisible, binding agreements with such unavoidable payments, but alas, Liv found a way around it by being my bestie."

"What about me?" Hemingway asked. "Am I now your servant for a hundred years?"

"You would be, but then I'd have to be around you, and that would crush my usually cheerful spirit," King Rudolf replied. "So I'll let you off the hook this time."

Hemingway heaved an overly dramatic sigh with relief. "Oh, good, because I'm sort of busy for the next one hundred years."

King Rudolf pointed at his mouth, giving Hemingway a stern expression. "Try to remember our agreement. No talky and you won't die-y."

CHAPTER SEVENTEEN

"He's an interesting person," Hemingway stated when King Rudolf made his exit.

"I'm fairly certain that he's both the smartest, most helpful person in the world and also was cursed to create headaches for all he encounters," Paris retorted.

"Well, thanks for your help." Hemingway flashed her a sideways smile. "I knew you'd have connections that might help, but I had no idea they'd be with the king of the fae."

"If that impresses you, wait until you meet my aunt," Paris bragged. "She's a leader of the dragonriders."

"Wow, you're pretty much royalty. I'm honored that you grace a peasant such as myself with your presence."

Paris playfully slapped Hemingway on the arm. "Don't be ridiculous. I'm the rebel outcast."

He winked at her. "I happen to like that about you."

Paris paid special attention to the seam between Heals Pills and the Rose Apothecary as she approached. She held up the card, wondering how this strange magic would work.

However, something else rather than the magical florist shop got her attention. Everyone on Roya Lane was on their phones. No one was paying attention to where they were going, all of them having their eyes glued to their device. She had noticed her attention stolen by her phone after Faraday enabled data to work at Happily Ever After College. However, knowing that she couldn't afford to lose valuable time to being addicted to it, she had locked it up in her room and thankfully forgotten about it.

It seemed that others on Roya Lane hadn't shown the same resistance to the technology. Many people were bumping into each other in their distracted states. Thankfully, most of the collisions didn't result in anyone getting harmed.

Striding out of Heals Pills was someone who Paris recognized and was glad to see alive. It wasn't entirely that she didn't believe Ramy Vance when he told her that he couldn't die easily—it was a strange concept. Falling into the fountain of youth had made it so he could keep coming back to life over and over again. The drawback to pretty much being bulletproof was that he was very clumsy and always bringing unfortunate accidents on himself.

The first time he'd died since she'd met him was very noble, saving Paris from the Deathly Shadow. However, she hadn't seen him die, so the next time she saw him, it wasn't that strange. On that occasion, Paris witnessed Ramy's death, which was disgusting and completely avoidable. Although she knew that he resurrected after every death, it was still surreal to see Ramy walking around after witnessing a large trashcan and its concrete holder crushing him.

Like everyone else, Ramy was glued to his phone, not paying attention to where he was walking. Unlike everyone else, the guy was headed straight for an open utility hole—making quick progress for the opening that had a dangerous drop.

"Ramy!" Paris yelled, hoping to get his attention before he took another step.

He glanced up as he extended his leg, hovering his foot right above the open hole in the road. His face brightened at the sight of Paris. "Hi, there!"

"Watch where you're going!" she yelled and pointed at him.

He gave her a thoughtful look. "Thanks, Paris. I definitely will." He looked around, but unfortunately not straight down. Then he nodded at her and waved. "See you later."

Ramy took another step and fell straight through the opening, landing with a gross *splat*.

Paris sighed, shaking her head. "What an avoidable and senseless death."

Hemingway bolted forward to the open utility hole and peered down into it. "Oh my God! He's dead!"

She nodded. "Don't worry. He'll be back to life in an hour or so."

"What?" Hemingway covered his gaze, trying to avoid looking at Ramy's dead body. "Are you serious?"

"Yeah, that's the third time he's died since I've known him," Paris explained.

"I guess the famous Hemingway was right as he said, 'Every man's life ends the same way. It is only the details of how he lived and how he died that distinguish one man from another.'"

"Yeah, and Ramy happens to die a lot."

"Wow, Roya Lane is a strange place."

"It is, and I think it's about to get stranger." Paris held up the golden card, and as King Rudolf had said, a shop shimmered to life between Heals Pills and the Rose Apothecary. Standing in plain sight but for only Paris and Hemingway to see was the Glowing Orchid, its front door open—welcoming them into the florist shop.

CHAPTER EIGHTEEN

"It's beautiful," Paris said in awe of the shop that had appeared in front of them.

Hemingway nodded, speechless as he took in the Glowing Orchid. The front display window was full of color with so many bright flowers filling every available space. There appeared to be an actual glow from the unique flowers that Paris had never seen before.

Wafting from the open door was an intoxicating scent. There was a gentle chiming sound that sounded like music, but Paris instinctively knew it wasn't.

She glanced at Hemingway. "Well, are you ready to find what you're looking for?"

"I think I've found my favorite place in the world." He didn't pull his gaze off the Glowing Orchid.

"Well, let's go shopping and find out what we need for trade." Paris strode for the open door.

Once she stepped over the threshold to the Glowing Orchid, she learned where the shimmering light was coming from. The name of the florist shop appeared to be literal. Sitting in the center of the store was a tiered display of various orchids, all of them giving off a glowing light. The breeze from Roya Lane gently followed the pair into the shop and shook the petals of the orchids, creating the chiming noise as if they were actual wind chimes hanging outside.

A woman with short black hair and kind eyes looked up from an arrangement she was putting together. "Oh, who did you get your invitation from?"

Paris held up the gold card. "King Rudolf Sweetwater."

Horror covered Astrid's face. "He's not with you, is he? It's taken a decade to clean up the mess from the last time he was in here."

"No, he sent us. I'm Paris, and this is my friend Hemingway. We're looking for something rare and unique and thought you could help."

Astrid nodded, relief replacing the worry. "You came to the right place. What are you looking for?"

Hemingway stepped forward, fascination in his eyes as he checked out the florist shop. "I'm looking for a flower to include in a memorial shrine. Something soft and yet strong. Timeless and symbolic of letting go."

"I know exactly what you'll need." Astrid snapped her fingers and held out her hand. A moment later, the strangest flower Paris had ever seen appeared in Astrid's fingers. The stem was thick, and that was probably necessary to hold up the large blossom on its end. The petals looked more like spiky strings and were the oddest color of blue. But the weirdest part of the flower was the center, which appeared like an architectural marvel with various structures protruding from the center. It was strangely beautiful and also otherworldly at the same time.

"May I present the passionflower," Astrid explained, holding out the bloom for Hemingway to inspect. His eyes showed his instant interest.

"It's incredible…and perfect…" he nearly stammered.

Astrid agreed with a nod. "Indeed it is."

"What do you need in trade for it?" Paris asked.

Astrid offered an appreciative smile. "I see you've learned that I don't accept money for purchases. Yes, I am looking for something in particular, but I'm not sure if you can help me with it. You see, my other passion is books. There's a particular one that's incredibly difficult to find called *The Clandestine Life of Plants.* It isn't in print, and no one that I've spoken to can find a copy."

"But there would be one in the Great Library," Paris said with a sudden rush of adrenaline.

Astrid nodded, disappointment on her face. "But I can't get in there."

"As a fairy godmother in training, I can," Paris stated proudly.

"Oh!" Astrid squealed. "You are? Really? A fairy godmother?"

"In training," Paris added, indicating herself and Hemingway. "We'll retrieve your book. Then can we have the flower?"

Astrid's face lit up. "Well, of course. I've long desired that book in my collection. How very fortuitous I asked you for the one thing you can get that none other has been able to. I'm really glad I had French toast this morning, or I might have asked for something else instead."

Paris scratched her head, surprised that King Rudolf had been right about the florist asking for certain things depending on what she had for breakfast. Everyone on Roya Lane was nuts…and awesome.

CHAPTER NINETEEN

"You realize that I can't get into the Great Library, right?" Hemingway said when they were back on Roya Lane. Again, almost everyone was glued to their phones, not paying attention to where they were going.

Paris tilted her head, confused. "Well, of course, you can. There's a portal entrance at Happily Ever After College."

He nodded. "It's for fairy godmothers and students to use for their studies."

"But you're a professor at the college."

Hemingway let out a disappointed sigh. "I teach, but I'm not faculty. I have some specialized knowledge and a free hour each day. Honestly, I'm only a glorified groundskeeper."

"You're not," Paris argued, not liking that Hemingway thought such a thing about himself. "You're important to the college, and the headmistress obviously values you."

"She does and is very supportive, but she can't change the rules," Hemingway explained. "Even Chef Ash can't get into the Great Library through the portal. Only fairy godmothers can cross that threshold."

"Well, that's dumb," Paris remarked. "You work for the college and should be able to get in there. Hell, why is it that fairy godmothers have to be females anyway? Why can't guys be ones? You know, like fairy godfathers."

He smiled, his blue eyes sparkling. "I love the way you think. It's definitely unlike most, but that kind of change at FGA might be impossible. The gender roles are pretty ingrained, and they expect everyone to stay in their lane."

"Well, put on a blinker, and let's shake some stuff up." Paris was excited about the idea of changing these roles—evolving them.

"If anyone can, it will be you," Hemingway said fondly. "But I don't think getting me into the Great Library is happening anytime soon, although I look forward to hopefully one day seeing that place. I've heard it's incredible."

"It is," Paris agreed. "I'll go retrieve the book for you. Hopefully, the Great Librarian will give me a copy. If he wants me to go retrieve something to trade, you'll hear me grumbling from the college."

Hemingway laughed. "As a fairy godmother, you should be able to get a copy."

"In training," she corrected again. "Hopefully it will be that easy. I swear, it always seems that with each mission, there's a mission within a mission."

"It does." Hemingway had to veer around people staring at their phones and not paying attention to where they were going. "Were you going to stop by the Official Brownie Headquarters while we're here?"

Paris shook her head, opening a portal to Happily Ever After College. "No, I'll do it after we complete this task for the shrine. Like you said, you have less of a window to do this before the planetary alignment."

"Thanks, Paris. This means a lot to me and knowing that I can trust you with what I'm doing, well, that's really meaningful."

"So do you think after this, you'll be ready to say farewell?"

Not hesitating, Hemingway nodded. "Absolutely. It's time, and it suddenly feels right, like something pushed me in the right direction after being stagnant for so long. It's as if someone came along and inspired me to take chances."

Paris couldn't help but blush, picking up on his subtle hint. "Well, I think you're very courageous to do this."

"Thank you." He looked at the portal shimmering ahead of them. "I'm glad you think so. And I'm grateful that Mae Ling has offered to help. I have a lot of wonderful people who are willing to help, but I couldn't do this without a very special one."

Paris' heart fluttered oddly—giving her a strange feeling in her chest she'd never experienced before. Covering up her nervousness and surprise, she stepped through the portal wondering if that's what butterflies felt like.

CHAPTER TWENTY

For over an hour, Paris strode through the Great Library, not encountering a single person. She was pretty sure she was lost in the rows and would perish in the expansive place. Paris hadn't attempted to find the book she was looking for, knowing that her library skills were probably lousy, not having spent hardly any time in one.

Paris had spent the hour trying to find the Great Librarian, Paul. She'd only ever been there once and didn't know if he sat at a reference desk or if she should look for his assistant, Beatrix the gryphowl —half owl and half cat. However, Paris didn't see any sign of either the librarian or his assistant and was worried she'd stay lost in the Great Library for the rest of her life.

She wished she'd brought a snack and looked around, longing for a Starbucks somewhere in that place like in those hip bookstores. Paris also regretted not grabbing her phone before she used the portal to the Great Library. If it worked in the bubble that was Happily Ever After College, then it must work wherever the library was.

However, she didn't have her phone. She was totally turned around and didn't know where the portal she'd come through was.

She considered doing a spell that might help her find her way, but it was hard to find the way when one doesn't know where they're going.

"Why is there no map in this place?" Paris muttered, wishing there was one of those displays that said, "You Are Here." Then she could at least know how lost she was, although a map still might not help her in a place this vast.

Almost as if saying it magically fulfilled her wish, she noticed carvings on the ends of the rows. She hadn't seen them before, but they were on each end. Closer inspection revealed that they were maps, to her surprise. It was almost as if they didn't appear until she asked for them. Or maybe it was like a theory in physics that Faraday was telling her about called the Observer Effect. Perhaps the maps didn't exist until Paris was there to observe them. Or by asking for them, she changed them.

However, to her disappointment she was right. The map didn't help her much because it was so detailed with all the various sections. However, it did show her where she was, which was a little blue dot. To her utter relief, there was another dot—this one red. It was labeled"The Great Librarian."

"Perfect." Paris sighed, deciphered the map, and took off in Paul's direction.

The Great Librarian wasn't close to Paris' location. She thought Paul must get a lot of exercise, working in the Great Library. He could probably benefit from a Segway or a golf cart to help him get around the humongous place.

Paris checked the maps on the ends of the rows several times to ensure she stayed headed in the right direction and that Paul hadn't moved. He hadn't.

Maybe he was napping. Paris laughed. The Great Library was a very relaxing place with all the rich wood and smell of books and silence.

When Paris finally found Paul, he wasn't asleep. To her surprise, he was on his phone, seemingly absorbed in a game she recognized as Wordscapes.

"Hey," she said, trying to get his attention.

"Hey," Paul replied absentmindedly, not startled by her sudden presence and not looking up from his phone. Paris could have been an ax murderer about to slaughter him, and he wouldn't have cared. Or worse, she could have held a torch to a book, and he wouldn't notice.

"I hoped that you could help me with something." Paris noticed how absorbed Paul was in the phone game.

"I'm glad you showed up when you did," Paul muttered, swiping his finger along as he made words from letters. "I need your help and will gladly do whatever you need in return."

"Yeah, of course," Paris replied. "What do you need?"

"I'm not sure, but something is definitely wrong," he answered. "I haven't read a book in days. No matter how I try, I can't pull my attention away from my phone."

Paris nodded. "Yeah, it's a growing problem, I've noticed. People on Roya Lane were obsessed with their phones when I was there. I had the same issue until I forced myself to lock it away."

"Please…take…it…from…me…and…destroy…it," Paul said in a pleading voice. He looked up, and there was such sadness in his eyes. Paris wondered if he'd slept or eaten since he was so engrossed in his phone.

She also sensed that he instantly regretted his request. He snatched his phone to the side as though trying to keep it away from her. Paris figured he might try to fight her when she took the device. The thing was, he could try, but she was certain she was faster and stronger, having arm-wrestled many a giant for fun. Her demon blood also gave her unmatched agility and power.

Thankfully Paul didn't try and fight her too much when in a blur, she shot forward and grabbed his phone. He screamed in pain and tried to yank it from her reach, but the effort was unsuccessful.

Paris backed up immediately before he could come after her, and in a flash, she threw the phone on the floor and slammed her boot down on it, crushing the device into countless broken pieces.

Horror filled Paul's face before he shook it off with a sober look. He sighed as though he'd run the length of the Great Library and caught his breath. "Thank you. I don't know what happened to me. You say this problem is widespread?"

Paris nodded, toeing the pieces of the device, looking for anything strange like magitech. It all seemed in order, but she knew who would have a better idea. She scooped up the pieces and put them in her jacket pockets. "Yeah, it appears that many are showing signs of being addicted to their phones."

Paul shuddered. "It was awful. I knew that I should be reshelving books or reading or any of my usual tasks, but all I wanted to do was be on my phone. It didn't matter what I was doing. I didn't think I could put the device down for long."

"There's definitely something nefarious going on," Paris remarked, thinking.

"Will you bring this to Headmistress Starr's attention?" Paul asked. "I think she should know about it and probably take it to FGA."

"Yes, of course." Paris got a strange inkling that like FriendNet, someone could be behind this phone business—but the question was, why? What did someone have to gain by making people addicted to their phones, not paying attention and getting into accidents, and unable to do their job properly? She didn't know, but she was going to find out.

"Now, you needed my help with something?" Paul asked. "I'm always happy to help a fairy godmother—"

"In training," Paris corrected once again.

"Yes, in training, but still," he replied. "And after prying that devilish phone from my grasp, I'm more indebted to you, Paris Beaufont. What may I assist you with?"

"I'm looking for a rare book called *The Clandestine Life of Plants*. Do you have it?"

He laughed proudly. "Do I have it? Of course. I have every book ever written…well, almost. A few have magical protections to prevent copying, but yes, I have that volume. Quite a fascinating read. I didn't know you had an interest in plants."

Paris hesitated for a moment. She didn't want to lie, and yet, if she told Paul the book was for someone else, would he be able to give it to her? Figuring that it was better to be honest, she cleared her throat. "It's not for me."

"Oh? A fellow student at Happily Ever After College?"

Paris shook her head.

"Maybe your Aunt Sophia, a dragonrider?" he questioned, seeming to want to supply her with a reason.

Another head shake. "No, it's no one who qualifies to be in the Great Library. I'm doing it for a trade for a special flower for a friend."

He lowered his chin, immediately crestfallen. "I'm not sure I can help you then, although I do appreciate your honesty."

"I realized that, but it's for a good reason, and I won't make a habit of getting rare books here for other people," Paris stated in a rush, trying to sound convincing.

"Well, as a fairy godmother—"

"In training," she cut in.

He nodded good-naturedly. "As a fairy godmother in training, your judgment is more aligned with good than most. I don't suspect that you'll give a dangerous book to the wrong person. Now, who is this volume for?"

"The shop owner of the Glowing Orchid," Paris answered, wondering if that was enough information. "It's on Roya Lane and—"

"Run by the one and only Astrid," Paul interrupted. "I had no idea she wanted that book, but it makes sense, and she would be unable to enter the Great Library."

"Yeah, do you think it will ever open up more so others can get in here?" Paris asked. "I mean, I get why it has to be restricted because knowledge is power. However, can't there be an ethics test that's given to people so they can qualify if they aren't a fairy godmother or a dragonrider or one of the others who can enter the Great Library?"

"That's a novel idea," Paul mused. "It's not up to me though. I don't make the rules. I simply must follow them."

"Then will you not be able to give me the book for Astrid?" Paris asked meekly.

He shook his head while snapping his fingers. "I don't see any reason that an expert horticulturist such as Astrid can't have this particular volume. I dare say, it belongs in her hands where it can benefit her and therefore the world at large."

A moment later, there was the sound of beating wings and a rush of air before Beatrix landed on Paul's outstretched arm. The two made eye contact, a message seeming to pass between them. As quickly as she'd arrived, the gryphowl sprang into the air.

Paul pointed in her direction. "Follow Beatrix, and she will lead you to the book you seek."

"Thanks." Paris set off at once, not wanting to lose the strange creature in the many rows that made up the Great Library. She also hoped the book wasn't very far, having already covered a lot of ground in the place that day.

CHAPTER TWENTY-ONE

The Clandestine Life of Plants was a huge book with tons of beautiful pictures and interesting little tidbits that Paris learned while glancing at the back cover. Like the fact that plants could talk to each other although each species spoke a different language and scientists couldn't decode most of them.

To her surprise, Paris discovered that many of the students in the fairy godmother mansion resembled those she'd seen on Roya Lane. Several had their heads down, engrossed with something on their phone.

Christine glanced up when Paris approached her in the hallway. "That sidekick of yours is the best. He fixed my phone—giving me access to data and messaging."

Paris' eyes widened with horror. "No, Faraday did what?"

"Hey, why should you be the only one who had a phone that works at Happily Ever After College?" Christine argued, scowling.

"Because there's a problem with the phones." Paris looked around and saw students sitting on the stairs or congregated in the hallways or open classrooms, all of them staring at their mobile devices. "He fixed everyone's phones?"

"Yeah, and I think he's now the most popular person...I mean, squirrel here at the college," Christine answered.

Paris sighed, trying to decide if she should pack her bags first or go and see Headmistress before that. She was pretty sure the meeting would end with her expulsion from Happily After College for Faraday's antics. After she packed and got expelled, she was going to turn the squirrel into a purse.

She knew he was trying to help, but he was also trying to make friends. She somewhat sympathized, knowing that Faraday hadn't had friends in his old life. However, not only did he enable phones to work at Happily Ever After College when they weren't supposed to, but he'd also done it when there appeared to be a spell making them demand users' attention.

Paris groaned. "I'm going to kill that squirrel."

"I hope you don't," Christine persuaded. "He's, like, the cutest creature in the world and so smart."

"And will probably taste excellent in a stew," Paris muttered.

"I don't think after everything he sacrificed to be with you that you can cook him," Christine sang, her eyes never moving from her device.

Paris huffed. "You think because he gave up a life as a human magician that I'm going to let this one go? The only place I thought was safe from whatever is happening with the phones was Happily Ever After College. Now it appears that the fairy godmothers are going down with the rest of the modern world."

"Oh, I got twenty 'likes' on my latest post on Instagram," Christine cheered. "Hollar_Back_Girl says that I'm hot."

Realizing that she had to face her fate, Paris trudged toward the headmistress' office.

CHAPTER TWENTY-TWO

"Oh, good, we were hoping that you'd stop by," Willow said when Paris knocked at her open office door.

Paris nodded. "I'll have my stuff packed and be gone by sunset."

The headmistress glanced at Mae Ling, who was sitting on the other side of her desk. Her expression was full of confusion, and she seemed to think the other fairy godmother could explain Paris' remark.

"We're not expelling you," Mae Ling said with confidence, seemingly reading her mind.

The headmistress gasped. "Oh, heavens no. Why would you think such a thing, Paris?"

"Because my squirrel programmed everyone's phones to work at Happily Ever After College," Paris explained, wondering if maybe Willow and Mae Ling didn't know about this yet and she was confessing.

Headmistress Starr pursed her lips and folded her hands on the surface of her neat desk. "Well, I can't say that wasn't a surprise. But if I'm honest, there isn't a good reason to prevent students from using their phones at the college. Communicating with family members and friends that can't visit here is important to me. The rule against technology was from a previous Saint Valentine's administration, and as you're aware, we're trying to weed out the old policies that keep us stuck."

"Oh, so I'm not in trouble for Faraday making the phones work?" Relief flooded Paris' chest.

"No, not in the least," Willow answered. "If Faraday hadn't updated the phones to work with all capabilities, we wouldn't have figured out what was affecting the love meter so quickly since we're admittedly in a bubble at Happily Ever After College."

Paris' gaze flew to the love meter hanging on the wall, and her heart plummeted as the love meter had. "What happened?"

It seemed that something was always bringing the dial on the love meter closer to zero after they fixed problems like what FriendNet caused.

"We think that whatever is happening with the phones is to blame," Mae Ling explained. "The problem appears to be widespread and started recently."

Paris combed her fingers through her hair. "Yeah, people on Roya Lane were like zombies, and Paul at the Great Library wanted me to bring it to your attention."

"Unfortunately, I'll have to confiscate all the phones on campus," Willow said regretfully. "But only until we remedy this situation. We can't have our students unable to focus because they're addicted to their devices."

"So people being obsessed with their phones is affecting the love meter," Paris guessed.

"That's what Saint Valentine supposes," Willow answered.

"It stands to reason that because couples are ignoring each other, spending all their time on their devices, that affection and love are down," Mae Ling imparted.

"Who or what do you think is behind this?" Paris thought about how strange it was that this was happening right after the debacle with FriendNet, which tried to break up many relationships.

"That's what we're going to need help with," Willow said. "Saint Valentine is keeping this very quiet at FGA. Understandably he doesn't trust his agents, even the ones in his office, Matters of the Heart. Although Agent Topaz will stand trial for Agent Opal's death and the murder attempt on Saint Valentine's life, he's still not taking any chances.

"Therefore, he doesn't want his agents looking into the problem with the phones. He came to me directly and asked if we could use our expertise to research. Then I learned that Faraday programmed the phones and it gave us a ray of hope."

"That's great that Saint Valentine is open to the idea that it could be Agent Ruby behind this—"

Willow held up her hand, pausing Paris. "Again, I heard your input on that, but there's no evidence pointing to Agent Ruby, and we can't accuse innocent people. Saint Valentine has decided not to trust any of his agents until after the trial. He's gone into hiding until after then."

"Well, then we need evidence," Paris said, mostly to herself, thinking that there were too many strange things going on. First, there were the mirrors at the FLEA jail and now the problem with the phones affecting the love meter. Something wasn't adding up, but she was going to figure it out.

"Do you think that Faraday can use his expertise to look into the issue with the phones?" Mae Ling recaptured Paris' attention.

"For sure," Paris said at once. "He's been looking for a mission to prove his worth. This is perfect, and if there is some sort of magitech or spell, he should be able to find out what it is. My uncle might also be able to help since he's savvy with magitech."

"Very good," Willow said with a pleasant smile. "I appreciate you helping out with this. I know that once again, it's unorthodox to have a student working on something of this magnitude, but let's be honest, you're not a typical student."

CHAPTER TWENTY-THREE

"So you're not going to turn me into a hat?" Faraday asked, looking over the pieces of Paul's phone that she'd brought back from the Great Library.

"I'm not going to today," she threatened. "I would have liked it if you asked me before you reprogrammed everyone's phone."

He nodded with shame in his eyes. "I'm sorry. It's just that I fixed Christine's phone and she was so happy, and it felt good. I've been hiding since I got here, but now that the headmistress is okay with my presence, well, it was nice to get out and talk to the students. Before too long, news spread about the phone, and everyone was asking."

"And you felt popular," Paris guessed.

"I felt needed and valuable, and that's more important," he corrected.

"Fair enough. Do you think you can figure out what's happening with the phones?"

"It's not a hardware issue." He picked through the pieces of the broken phone with his paws.

"So not magitech then?" Paris questioned.

"I don't think so," Faraday answered. "I think it's a powerful broadcasting spell. It would work on humans and not animals because I hadn't had any problems when programming the students' phones."

Paris pondered this. "So it's a spell that's using the phone signals, you think?"

"It's too early for me to tell," he cautioned. "I need to run a few experiments before I advise."

"Do you think that if you figure out what it is, you can fix it?"

"I don't want to get your hopes up," Faraday answered. "Let me look into it first, and we'll see. If I can reverse it, I'll try."

"However, that won't do us much good unless we figure out who is behind it and how to prevent them from doing it again," Paris stated.

"We both have our suspicions about who could be behind this," Faraday said pointedly.

"You think it's Agent Ruby?" Paris did too, but she wanted it to come from someone else so she didn't sound like a conspiracy theorist.

"We're fairly certain that he's the one who orchestrated the relationship problems with FriendNet," Faraday began. "When that failed, it stands to reason that he looked for another way to bring the love meter down."

"But why would an FGA agent want love to plummet?" Paris tried to work out the details.

"Why would an FGA agent want Saint Valentine dead?" Faraday countered.

"Because the board and many agents are adamantly and outwardly disapproving of his modern and radical practices," she answered, thinking.

Faraday flicked his tail. "Since we're assuming that Agent Ruby was the one who orchestrated the issues with FriendNet, it stands to reason that he did so to bring the love meter down."

"Using technology and social media, which Saint Valentine supports," Paris offered.

"Which would make him and his office look bad," Faraday added.

Her eyes widened at the implications of all they were piecing together. She'd been on the precipice of all these assumptions, but now they were weaving together. "Using phones to make relationships deteriorate is pretty much the same idea, with similar results."

Faraday chirped, his whiskers twitching. "It seems that Saint Valentine shares our suspicions of his FGA agents if he's not sharing information about this with them."

"If it is Agent Ruby behind FriendNet, he could be the one who tried to murder Saint Valentine," Paris said in a rush.

"I think we have to be careful jumping to that assumption," Faraday warned. "The headmistress is right, and we need evidence. You can loosely link Agent Ruby to FriendNet, but that's not enough to convict him. We know there are many at FGA who want the current Saint Valentine out of office. What you need is to investigate and get more information. A good hypothesis is a start, but worthless unless tested, producing evidence to support your case."

Paris nodded, making for the door to her bedroom. "Okay, I'll see what I can dig up, and you research the phone situation. We'll reconvene when we both have more information."

Faraday chuckled, looking amused. "I like that you, the halfling, are doing the digging. And me, the squirrel, is doing the research."

She joined him, laughing too. "Yeah, it's a good reverse-y world, for sure."

CHAPTER TWENTY-FOUR

"So your squirrel is the reason that no one was paying attention in my class today," Hemingway said as they stepped onto Roya Lane.

"No, some evil mastermind who is trying to sabotage love for unknown purposes is the reason," Paris argued.

"Still, none of the students had phones that could message or use data at Happily Ever After College before Faraday," Hemingway countered.

"True, but he's also going to try and work out what's happening and hopefully fix it." Paris handed the book she'd obtained from the Great Library to Hemingway. "The gold invitation card is inside the first page of this, in case you need that to make the Glowing Orchid appear again. I don't know, it might be like a standing invitation and once we're allowed entry, then we can always."

A look of disappointment crossed Hemingway's face. "You're not going with me to see Astrid?"

"I would," she began, "but I need to find the Official Brownie Office. This whole business with the phones makes me worried, and with the planetary alignment approaching, I need to find all the mirrors. What if Agent Topaz is having someone help him escape?

There are too many questions at this point, and I promised Faraday I'd find evidence."

Hemingway nodded understandingly. "Yeah, and I've already demanded enough of your time with this whole thing."

"No, you didn't demand anything," she countered. "I'm honored that you asked for my help. Now we've learned about the Glowing Orchid and met Astrid. Who knows how that could come in handy in the future."

"It's deadly helpful in my profession," a familiar voice said behind Paris, obviously having been eavesdropping.

She whipped around to find Lee, the baker from the Crying Cat Bakery, standing with her arms crossed and a cunning expression. "Oh, hey. You know about the Glowing Orchid?"

"Know about it?" Lee challenged, combing her fingers through her short curly hair. "I probably single-handedly keep Astrid in business."

"Oh, because you source plants for your baked goods from there?" Paris guessed.

A laugh burst out of Lee's mouth. "Yeah, I used the magical and exotic plants in my brownies and not to create poisons."

Hemingway tilted his head. "Oh, I guess you're the assassin baker who King Rudolf threatened to have come after me if I kept talking."

Lee pointed at him. "You're Hemingway? Oh, good to meet you. We have an appointment tomorrow to meet again. Well, I'll meet you, and you'll meet a blunt object."

Paris waved her hands. "No. No. You're not killing Hemingway."

"But King Rudolf asked nicely and offered to buy me a yacht," Lee pouted.

"You live on Roya Lane and not the sea," Paris argued.

Lee waved her off. "Such limited thinking. Ships don't have to be on the water."

"Oh, silly me." Paris laughed.

"Can we get back to that whole me being assassinated thing?" Hemingway looked between the two.

Lee pursed her lips at him. "You're one of those people who make everything about you. No wonder the king wanted you dead."

"I thought it was because I was handsome and talked too much," Hemingway said. "And I quit talking. That's not fair that he still put the hit on me. If I knew that, I would have kept chatting him up. If I'm dying, I'm going out my way."

Paris stuck hands on her hips. "Lee, you're not killing Hemingway. Tell Rudolf I said that and if he wants Hemingway dead because he's attractive, I'm never talking to him again."

"What about my boat?" Lee asked.

"Forget about the boat," Paris urged.

"But I bought a captain's hat."

Paris glanced at Hemingway. "On second thought, I'm going with you to the Glowing Orchid. I'm not sure I should let you out of my sight until I see my pseudo uncle and punch him in the face."

Lee nodded proudly. "That's how I communicate with my uncle too. Sweet family traditions."

Hemingway held out his arm to Roya Lane. "Well, I'm not going to argue if you, the beautiful and brave Paris Beaufont, want to be my bodyguard while an assassin heads to the same place as me. Especially one who has a hit out on me thanks to your wacky uncle."

CHAPTER TWENTY-FIVE

"You brought what I asked for," Astrid blurted when the three entered the Glowing Orchid. Her eyes were bright with excitement, and she looked ready to jump up and down.

Lee nodded and pulled a bag of jelly beans from her pants pocket. "That's right. I got you the silly beans that don't only taste good but ensure you have a good Saturday night, if you know what I mean." She winked at the horticulturist, who waved her off and angled toward Hemingway, who was holding the prized book—*The Clandestine Life of Plants.*

"You got what I've been looking for most of my life," Astrid murmured. "Not only can you have what you asked for, the passion-flower, but you have my protection, and any who ever harm you will forever be my enemy."

Lee threw her arms up to the ceiling, looking at the rafters. "Fine, fine, fine. I won't kill Romeo. I can't have my supplier hating me. That would put me out of business."

Astrid glanced over her shoulder at the assassin baker momentarily before shaking her off. She turned back to Hemingway and pointed at the large book in his arms. "May I?"

He nodded at once, placing the volume in her hands. "Yes, and it looks fascinating with plant behavior that I never knew existed. I mean, at Happily Ever After College, I've observed reverse pollinations thanks to pixie magic and bipolar disorder in plants, but only rarely. This book details it all."

Astrid glanced up from the book, her face full of surprise. "It sounds like you know your plants."

"What he needs to know is how to pretend to be dead." Lee smelled a bright red flower with a yellow tendril snaking around in the air. "If he did, I'd get a boat, and he could live, albeit incognito."

"I'm not pretending to be dead," Hemingway said. "I feel like I'm living for the first time, finally venturing outside to Roya Lane."

"I'm glad to hear you say that." Astrid slid the new book into a cupboard and shut and locked it at once with a protective expression. "I've been looking for someone to contract for a little while. I need an employee who can travel around, searching in exotic locations for plants that I can keep in my shop. It needs to be someone with an appetite for adventure and knowledge of magical plants. What do you say?"

Hemingway looked like he'd swallowed a frog and jerked his gaze at Paris as though expecting her to help him with an answer. She shrugged, not sure what to say.

Recovering, he offered Astrid a hesitant smile. "Thanks for the offer. I'm happy at the college right now, but I'll definitely keep that in mind. It's an intriguing offer for when I decide to spread my wings."

"Your fake wings, you mean," Lee stated, making everyone's head jerk up.

The assassin put her finger to her mouth and winked. "Don't worry, magician. Your secret is safe with me. Astrid won't talk because, well, she doesn't. No one hardly even knows her shop exists."

Astrid nodded, giving Hemingway a consoling look. "I won't say anything. I'm sure you have a good reason."

"I do," Hemingway stated. "With that, may I please have the passionflower? I have a short window of time to create the memorial shrine."

"Of course." Astrid held out her hand. A moment later, the bright blue flower appeared in it, looking both delicate and also sturdy. "Once put into place, it won't ever wilt or die. From the moment you place it, the passionflower will always look the same, but it's important that you hurry and arrange it right away. That's best to preserve its integrity."

"Oh, okay," Hemingway said with surprise, taking the flower. He glanced at Paris, and she ushered him toward the door.

"I'll meet you back at the college once I finish here," she encouraged.

He nodded, backing for the door. "Yes, I'd like you there for the ceremony, if you wouldn't mind. It wouldn't be happening without you."

She smiled and waved him toward Roya Lane. "I'll be there as soon as I can."

"Okay, thanks." Hemingway left with the passionflower without another word.

Lee turned to Astrid with a sneaky grin. "Well, I came for a dose of love from the sweetheart flower, but it appears that I've already gotten a dose of that through osmosis."

CHAPTER TWENTY-SIX

Paris felt like a loon, standing in front of a solid brick wall on Roya Lane and facing it as others passed on the cobbled street. The only thing that made it feel better was that none of the passersby were paying her the slightest bit of attention since they were all looking at their phones.

Paris' mother had given her that specific location for the Official Brownie Headquarters, but it seemed strange that the door was there and yet not there. She didn't know why this was so hard to comprehend. After all, Paris went to college in an unmapped bubble, and no one knew where it was. However, it was strange to Paris that this brick wall that she passed a thousand times in her life might hold a door to an office for house elves. She swallowed her hesitation and cleared her throat.

"This is Paris Beaufont, fairy godmother in training to see the leader of the Brownies, Mortimer."

Nothing happened, making Paris think that maybe she had the location wrong. She didn't have exact coordinates. Paris reasoned that in fifteen years, things might have changed.

As she considered trying something else, a small door shimmered to life in the brick wall. It was a really small door, made for someone who was only about two feet tall. Paris glanced around, wondering if another door might open that was her size. When one didn't, she tried the tiny handle and poked her head through tentatively.

"Hello," she called, spying a long corridor, although it also had low ceilings. "Paris Beaufont here."

"Please come through Paris Beaufont," a squeaky voice sang, "fairy godmother in training for Happily Ever After College. I have so many questions for you."

CHAPTER TWENTY-SEVEN

Paris honestly thought her hips were stuck when she tried to wiggle through the narrow Brownie door. She was grateful that no one could see her trying to push her butt through the small opening to the office—at least she hoped no one had lined up for that front row show.

When she had finally managed to arrive in the Official Brownie Headquarters, the sight was a bit underwhelming. There was an impeccably kept but lackluster reception office, a long hallway with no effects, and a slightly ajar door at the far end.

"Down here, Paris Beaufont," the squeaky voice said excitedly from the other end of the hallway.

Deciding that nothing that regularly used the door she'd come through could be dangerous, Paris started down the hallway.

She knocked on the half-open door, deciding she wasn't interrupting at this point. "I'm here."

"Come in and let me look at you," the squeaky voice said.

Paris pushed it wide, not sure what she was expecting to see since she'd never seen a Brownie—as most hadn't. She'd heard about them, but even in the magical world, they were considered more myth than real.

What she saw wasn't so far outside of her realm of possibilities but also wasn't normal in the real world. The Brownie sitting in the high-backed chair was halfway between a businessman in the mortal world and a hairy, adorable creature that resembled a tiny elf without all the hippie ways.

The leader of the Brownies, apparently known as Mortimer, was wearing a very tailored business suit, his tie tight around his neck. He'd slicked back the hair on his head, and the rest on his body was too, but not as much. His long ears perked up, and his large eyes shone with excitement.

"You look just like her." He popped up to his feet, his height not changing at all.

She ducked into the office, keeping her head low so she didn't hit it. "You mean my mother?"

"Yes," he chirped. "Liv Beaufont, Warrior for the House of Fourteen. She was by far the best magician I've had the pleasure of meeting. Although Sophia Beaufont, second in command for the Dragon Elite and the leader of the Rogue Riders, is a very close second and I always enjoy every opportunity I get to see her."

Paris, not knowing how such meetings went, bowed, careful not to rise all the way when she finished. "Well, it's a pleasure to meet you. My mother told me that you might be able to help."

Mortimer's eyes widened. He squealed and covered his mouth, looking like he might jump up and down. "Did you say that your mother told you…as in present time? As in recently? As in you have spoken to Liv Beaufont, Warrior for the House of Fourteen?"

Paris looked around, guessing it was okay to be honest since Liv said Mortimer could be trusted. She had sent Paris to him after all. "She's back," Paris began in a low voice. "But she and my father are recovering at the Fantastical Armory, and no one is to know they are back until they're ready."

He nodded, delight heavy in his eyes. "This secret is safe with me. It makes sense that I didn't know about it if they're at the Fantastical Armory. This is a wonderful day to be alive. A wonderful decade. Century, I'd say. If Liv is returning, well, things will be great once more. She'll police that which needs policing. She'll help that which needs help. Your father will control the demon population. It will all go back to normal. Well, the normal that we all took for granted when they ruled."

"Ruled" sounded like Paris came from royalty. That was so hard for her to comprehend. Still, she nodded, having trouble following this tiny little guy who had more energy than the Energizer Bunny times ten.

"I'm sure that once my parents are back, they will be here to see you," Paris began diplomatically. "My mother sent me to you. She said you might be able to help me with something because you have eyes and ears everywhere."

He nodded excitedly. "That I do. It's nice to hear that you're going down the same path as your mother and aunt. They are what keeps this world going around."

Paris swallowed. "Well, I wouldn't put me in the same league as them. I'm a fairy godmother in training."

"Which will soon make you a fairy godmother," Mortimer interrupted.

Paris shrugged. "If I pass my exams and wear a dress and pretty much sell my soul."

"Well, what can I do to help you, Paris Beaufont, fairy godmother in training?"

"I hear that you and the Brownies can get into most places, right?"

"Yes, most places," he answered. "With the exception of places like the Fantastical Armory."

She nodded. "And because your specialty is cleaning, you see things that remain hidden from others."

"What is it that you need us to clean up?" Mortimer looked up for the challenge.

"We think that someone is placing mirrors in the FLEA jail area."

"In time for the planetary alignment," he guessed.

Paris nodded. "Do you think you can help clean them up?"

For the first time since they'd met, his enthusiastic expression dropped. "I can try. I'll put my Brownies to the task. We can probably get most of them…probably."

"But…" Paris sensed his hesitation.

"Mirrors are hard for us to see," he explained. "There's a magic that can hide them that's hard to spot. It's because of how they work, reflecting things that make them easier to hide even from us. I'm certain we can find most of them, Paris Beaufont, fairy godmother in training at Happily Ever After College. But I must warn you that we may not be able to locate all of them."

"What will that mean if someone is using them to hide something?" All of this was new to Paris.

"It means they or whatever they're hiding will remain partially hidden during the planetary alignment. Hopefully, there will be big gaps where you can see them, but first, we must get in there and do the work for you. I promise to try and clean up the jail as best we can."

Paris smiled, grateful to have such helpful people to assist her. It proved that her mother had the best friends in the world.

CHAPTER TWENTY-EIGHT

"What in the name of Cupid is going on here?" Paris halted as soon as she entered her room. That was mostly because she couldn't take another step farther. The already small room was cramped with wires, monitors, and various other technical pieces of equipment. Even stranger than finding her room looking like a computer from the 1980s was that Faraday was sitting on what used to be her bed and typing on three different keyboards with his front two paws and one back leg, putting him in quite the precarious position.

Almost weirder than that was Wilfred, the magitech AI butler, standing in the only available space in the room and holding a thick cable. Electricity radiated around his hands and the cord.

Faraday hurriedly glanced up. "Oh, I had to build a supercomputer of sorts to track down the signal broadcasted to the phones."

"Why does Wilfred look like he's a conduit that's close to being fried?" Paris was afraid to touch anything for fear of electrocution.

Faraday tapped decisively on the keyboard before turning to face Paris. "Because he is. But I have everything under control."

Wilfred nodded. "Yes, once we put out the fire, there haven't been any other issues."

"Fire?" Paris questioned, sniffing and smelling the residual smoke in the air. "There was a fire in here."

"Yes," Faraday chirped. "Remember how you kept saying that you needed to get rid of those old combat boots that are your second pair?"

"Yes," she drew out the word.

"Well, now you don't have to," he proudly said as if he'd done her a great favor by catching her room on fire and taking it over with electronics.

"Fare…" She looked around and noticed singe marks covering her dresser. She didn't think she'd ever get the campfire smoke smell out of her t-shirts.

"Yes, Pare?" Faraday blinked at her.

"Not that I mind," she began, "but do you think that since the college knows about you now and you're technically working for them—"

His eyes widened with horror. "You want me to move out of your room!"

Paris shook her head. "No, I wonder if there's an available space that you could use as your lab for future projects."

"I think that's a good idea," Wilfred stated in his usual dignified tone, although he was vibrating with electricity. It surged more with each passing second, making Paris worry he might explode, although she wasn't sure if that was possible.

"My own lab!" Faraday exclaimed with excitement. "That would be fantastic. Wilfred was able to get a lot of this equipment from when the fairy godmothers were creating the magitech staff members."

"The ones that didn't work," Paris added.

"Yes," Faraday confirmed. "That's the reason I've had to create a hodgepodge computer of sorts, but I think it works well enough for my purposes."

"I see no reason that the headmistress won't purchase whatever technology you might need for this lab," Wilfred stated.

"Really!" Faraday squealed. "That would be a dream come true."

"Well, if you fix the catastrophe happening with the phones worldwide or at least offer a solution, I think Headmistress Starr will see how valuable it will be to have your services on hand for other further issues," Wilfred explained. "I mean, technological advancements are the way the college is going under the current administration."

"Not if someone has a say about it," Paris muttered, thinking of Agent Ruby, who she suspected was behind all this more and more, but she still needed proof. She indicated the contraption taking over her room. "So until you have a lab, has this worked out what's happening with the phones?"

Faraday nodded, going back to typing on the various keyboards, making images flash onto the screens. "I was able to take your phone and isolate a unique signal it was receiving that shouldn't be a part of the normal programming. Using a world map simulator—"

"Can we get to the part where you speak English, and I follow you?" Paris interrupted.

"Right," he chirped. "There's a satellite broadcasting a signal to all mobile devices that I believe is the culprit. It has a strange code that I haven't deciphered, but my hunch is that spell work riddles it."

"Great!" Paris clapped. "Where's the switch? How do we turn off this sinister signal making everyone addicted to their phones?"

"That's the tricky part." Faraday tipped his head back and forth.

"That's the tricky part?" she asked sarcastically. "It wasn't you destroying my room to create a supercomputer to determine there's a signal trespassing into phones?"

He waved her off dismissively. "That wasn't that difficult. The satellite, as best as I can determine, is located in the thermosphere. I need to be closer to it to hack the signal it's broadcasting and shut it off."

"You can't do it from here?" Paris waved at the screens. "With the monster computer you've built?"

"I'm afraid not," he answered. "I need to be higher up. Closer to the satellite."

"Great, so we need to haul your giant computer to the rooftop then?"

Faraday shook his head. "Higher."

Paris lowered her chin. "Like, how high?"

The squirrel offered an odd grin of sorts. "I guess you'd say that the switch to shut off the signal is in the sky."

"How high up do you need to be?" Paris looked between the squirrel and the butler, noticing they both wore uncertain expressions.

"At least in the stratosphere," Wilfred answered, cutting into the conversation.

"Which is where?" Paris questioned.

Wilfred was still holding the electric cable. "It's the level that planes fly at."

"Great." Paris was ready to get this going and the phones fixed. The love meter was dangerously low, and it was getting worse the longer people stayed addicted to their phones. Relationships weren't the only thing at stake. People were in danger and neglecting their lives in so many ways. "What do you want me to grab? We'll charter a plane and put this device on it. I'm sure that Willow will sign off on whatever will fix the problem."

"A plane won't work." Faraday's expression turned apologetic.

"Why not?" Paris thought she'd probably regret asking.

"Because the navigational software will interfere with what I have to do to take down the signal," the squirrel answered.

"Well, I don't think this giant computer will fit on a hot air balloon," Paris remarked.

"I should be able to use a regular laptop with a big processor," Faraday explained. "This computer was so I could detect the signal and pinpoint it. Now I have the coordinates, and we only have to be close-ish."

"Right, in the stratosphere." Paris laughed, a little surprised she was having this conversation with a squirrel who seemed about to fix a major global problem...with a laptop and a hot air balloon.

Faraday flicked his tail like he did when nervous. "My research has also discovered a problem that we need to prepare for when shutting down the signal."

"Why am I not surprised," Paris said dryly.

"It appears that whoever set up the signal protected it from getting turned off—"

"Almost as if they expected that someone would figure it out," Paris interrupted the squirrel.

"Defensive measures are usually put into place when people know they are doing something deceitful," Wilfred offered.

"What are these defensive measures?" Paris asked.

"There appear to be drones stationed around the satellite in the mesosphere, and I'd guess they're armed and ready to fire at threats," Faraday explained.

"So a hot air balloon won't work then."

Faraday shook his head.

Paris folded her arms over her chest. "I'm guessing the mesosphere separates the stratosphere from the thermosphere."

"Very good!" Faraday exclaimed, his eyes dancing with sudden excitement.

"I'm not becoming a science nerd so pipe down," she fired. "I'm trying to figure out how we're going to deal with this."

Wilfred cleared his throat in a dignified manner, politely gaining their attention. "It seems as though someone knew that to shut down the signal broadcasting to the phones, proximity would be a requirement. They therefore stationed these drones to protect the satellite."

"Can we fire a missile at the satellite?" Paris thought she'd come up with the solution. "No hot air balloon and no worries that this villain will restart the signal."

"Although a clever idea," Faraday began, "first, I believe that I can stop the signal and corrupt the satellite so this doesn't happen again."

"Well, until this person finds another satellite," Paris stated.

The squirrel chewed a few times on nothing. "I hope that you or someone finds who is behind this before that can happen. Second, finding a missile with that kind of range and accuracy will be difficult. Not only that, but it could take some time."

Paris nodded. "And time is of the essence. We need to stop this signal yesterday, which means we'll leave military forces out of it. I can only imagine the bureaucratic red tape to get access to a long-range missile."

The room fell silent, everyone momentarily showing expressions of defeat.

Faraday tapped on the keyboard, his eyes perplexed. Wilfred continued to hold the cable buzzing with electricity. Paris drummed her fingers on her pursed lips, thinking.

"So we need to get you up high enough to the satellite with a computer, but it can't be on a plane," she said, mostly talking to herself and trying to work out a solution. "And however we get you up there, we need to be prepared for an attack from the guard drones. So we need something that flies, is tough, and can defend you while you shut down the signal."

Faraday's eyes widened suddenly, and a squeal of excitement fell from his mouth.

Seemingly reading his thoughts, Paris popped a hand to her mouth to muffle the exhilaration falling from her lips.

"You two have both silently figured out an option," Wilfred guessed, looking between the pair.

Faraday nodded. "I think it could work. Do you think they will help?"

Paris smiled wide. "They have to be aware of the problem and are probably looking for a solution the same as us. I bet they'll be chomping at the bit to help."

"Would it be too much to ask that you two divulge the solution you've found?" Wilfred asked. "I'm experiencing a rare moment of curiosity."

"Well, that's progress and hopefully paves the road to one day laughing at my jokes, Wil." Paris slapped her hands together victoriously. "We're going to use one of my connections to ensure Faraday can safely and effectively shut down the signal the satellite is broadcasting."

Wilfred glanced at Faraday, seeing the squirrel's tail flicker repeatedly with excitement.

Faraday grinned, his eyes eager. "I'm going to complete two life-long dreams. The first is to do something scientific that globally helps the human race. Second, to ride a real dragon."

CHAPTER TWENTY-NINE

"So this is what Beverly Hills looks like," Faraday muttered, his words partly muffled.

Paris peered down into the duffle bag she had slung over her shoulder where Faraday was curled up, unable to see anything. "Oh, you're not missing anything. Only fancy cars and big houses. You see one, and you've seen them all."

"Are there any Teslas? I'd rather like to get under the hood of one of those," the squirrel said excitedly.

Paris strode down the sidewalk, offering a polite smile to a couple who gave her a curious look for talking to herself. "You being in the bag was supposed to make me not look like a loon, but it's not working."

"Probably because it's who you are and you can't hide that."

"Ha-ha," she said humorlessly, pausing at a crosswalk and looking both ways before proceeding. "Well, because people already think I look insane, I didn't need a talking squirrel following me down the sidewalk too. I can't afford for you to get run over. You're supposed to save the world, remember?"

"Yes, I haven't forgotten," Faraday sang from the bag. "It does sound busy out there on the street."

Paris hurried down the last stretch of sidewalk to the Rogue Riders' Mansion. "Yeah, the fumes are a gross contrast from the clean air at Happily Ever After College."

"It is, but the pollen in the air there messes with my seasonal allergies," Faraday offered.

Paris shook her head. "You're the strangest squirrel in the history of rodents."

Rounding the corner, Paris nearly ran down the long driveway to the large house in the distance. She hoped that Sophia was home. Ironically, she couldn't send her a message that she was coming because she didn't want to start the addiction for her aunt if she hadn't been affected yet. Paris hoped that Lunis and Sophia would be available to help, but if not, she'd have to convince one of the other Rogue Riders to assist.

To Paris' relief, many of the riders and dragons were lined up on the expansive lawn, standing at attention as their leader strode back and forth.

"It's come to my attention that many of you have been slacking on your responsibilities lately, too engrossed in your mobile devices," Sophia Beaufont said, her chin in the air and her tone full of authority.

Beside her the blue dragon sighed, smoke issuing from his nostrils. "I'll have you know that harvesting my orchards on Animal Crossing is part of my responsibilities. And those fish aren't going to catch themselves."

Sophia glared at her dragon. "For once, I'm not talking about you slacking on the job, Couch Potato."

"Ouch." Lunis feigned hurt from the remark by the tiny little human he could crush with a flick of a toe—although Paris' money was still on Sophia.

The Rogue Riders appeared close to bursting with laughter but were well-practiced at remaining stoic when Lunis and Sophia bantered.

Catching sight of Paris approaching with the duffle bag, Sophia's face brightened with a smile. "Oh, I didn't expect you!"

Paris hurried, making up the distance. "Yeah, sorry to interrupt, but it seems like the timing might be good."

"How so?" Sophia tilted her head in confusion.

"Well, I think I can tell you why your riders are preoccupied with their phones," Paris explained. "It's why I'm here. I need your help. There appears to be a signal that's broadcasting to all mobile devices, making people obsessed with them."

"See!" Lunis exclaimed. "It's not my fault. I've been brainwashed."

Paris glanced at the blue dragon. "Sorry to say, but it only works on humans."

"And?" Lunis questioned, drawing out the word.

Sophia shook her head at him. "You're a dragon."

His mouth popped open as if he was suddenly offended. "Don't limit me, Sophia Beaufont. I happen to be dabbling in some transformation magic. If I can turn myself into a human, that opens up the dating options on Bumble. No one swipes right on a dragon anymore."

"Can you blame them?" Sophia asked. "You breathe fire and have spikes."

He huffed. "The real problem is that most restaurants won't seat me. It's discrimination."

Sophia shook her head, returning her attention to Paris. "What is going on? There's a signal broadcasting to the phones? My riders weren't slacking on the job?" She indicated the riders and dragons still standing at attention but very interested in the conversation, many leaning closer.

"No, I think that was a mastermind who created it to destroy relationships," Paris explained. "People are all ignoring each other, and the result is that the love meter is down."

Sophia combed her hand over her chin while thinking. "I saw reports of more accidents linked to mobile use, but that's been on the rise for a while."

"I think that's a residual effect," Paris stated. "But you definitely would have seen a spike, and it's only going to get worse."

"So you need the Rogue Riders' help to fix this problem?" Sophia asked. "We're definitely in. What can we do?"

Paris shook her head. "I think we'll need one dragon's help. I have a plan, thanks to my scientist friend." She felt Faraday squirm around in the bag but thought it better to delay his reveal until the right moment.

"I'm it!" Lunis cheered. "If one dragon gets picked to fix humans being obsessed with their phones and that is bringing love down, it's sooooo me." The dragon stuck his tongue out at the others. "Take that! That's the perk of being in charge, suckers!"

Sophia smirked at her dragon. "I'm wondering when maturity is also going to go along with you being in charge."

"Hard to say," Lunis muttered. "I always have to overcompensate for my co-leader's stuffiness. She's so uptight that—"

"Finish that sentence, and I'll transform you into a mutt and drop you off at the pound," Sophia interrupted.

"Do you see the abuse I endure?" Lunis asked Paris, looking hurt.

She covered her laughter. "I'd hold off on the transformation spells. I've heard they can backfire."

"They definitely can," Lunis agreed. "One time Sophia turned me into a rat, and I still have an unhealthy obsession with cheese."

"Which was the same before the transformation," Sophia added.

"But now I have an excuse!" Lunis sang.

Sophia shook her head and glanced at Paris. "So you need a dragon, and I'm guessing a rider. You say that your scientist friend has a solution? I'm so impressed that you're on this case and already saving the world. Your mother..." Sophia's gaze drifted to the riders who were still listening. "Well, you know that she'd be proud."

Paris nodded, knowing that what she meant was that she was proud, but no one knew that Liv and Stefan were back yet. Hopefully, Sophia and Clark would be able to see them soon, and then they'd be that much closer to getting back to normal.

"Thanks," Paris replied. "Yes, my friend detected the signal and knows how to stop it. But he needs to be closer to the satellite in the thermosphere."

"I live in the stratosphere," Lunis cut in.

Paris giggled. "And we've decided that the safest way to bring down the signal would be on a dragon because of technological complications and also…well, drones are guarding the satellite."

"Oh, I loathe drones," Lunis remarked.

"So you need transportation and a defense," Sophia guessed.

"That's right," Paris affirmed.

"We get your scientist friend close enough, deflect the attacks from the drones, and he can stop the signal?" Sophia asked.

"Yes, and the world will go back to normal," Paris added.

Sophia pursed her lips at her riders. "Then you all won't have an excuse for slacking."

"Well, not until the next mastermind concocts a plan to bring down love," Lunis remarked.

"I'm trying to find out who is behind this evil scheme and bring them to justice," Paris said with passion.

Sophia's face filled with pride. "I probably don't have to tell you this, but those are words of a real Beaufont. Justice and the need to preserve it is printed on our soul."

"That's weird." Lunis laughed. "I think there's something wrong if you have a print on your soul. Maybe you should ask Mama Jamba for a return."

Sophia shook her head and tried to focus, which the blue dragon didn't make easy. "Your friend. This scientist. Where is he? As soon as we get specifics from him on the location, we can get going."

Paris stifled her nervousness as she reached into the bag and retrieved Faraday. She held the squirrel in the air and grinned. "Please meet the scientist who is going to save the world—his name is Faraday."

CHAPTER THIRTY

"Oh! My! Gods!" Lunis gushed. "Can I keep him, Soph? You know how much I've been asking for a squirrel who is good at science!"

Sophia, definitely surprised by the reveal, shook her head. "No, you already have a hedgehog."

Lunis sighed over the reactions of the Rogue Riders, who also appeared shocked by Faraday. "My hedgehog is totally boring. All he does is eat and sleep and well, you know."

"And he probably can't do complex trigonometry," Faraday said, hanging limply in Paris' hand.

"He talks!" Lunis screamed, looking like he might faint from excitement. "Name your price, Paris. No amount is too much. Your aunt is rich, and I have access to her bank accounts."

"He's not for sale," Paris replied.

"You're the talking squirrel," Lunis said. "Faraday! We're going to be the best of friends. You can gather nuts for me—"

"He's allergic to nuts," Paris interrupted.

"Well, you can climb trees, and I'll watch you jump from branch to branch—"

"He doesn't like trees or jumping or doing pretty much anything that's squirrel-like," Paris imparted.

Lunis deflated. "Alas, I have to return the talking squirrel you gave me. He's defective. I'll take my refund in cash."

"I apologize for my dragon's…well, mental disorder is the best way I can put it." Sophia offered Faraday a welcoming smile.

"He's fascinating," Faraday nearly stuttered, his eyes wide. "Do all dragons have a similar demeanor?"

"No, those guys are all a big yawn fest," Lunis answered, pointing a claw at the row of dragons all glaring at him.

"Lun is pretty special in his uniqueness," Sophia offered.

"So can you help us?" Paris asked, trying to steer the conversation back on track. "Faraday would need the ride to the stratosphere."

"How much do you weigh?" Lunis asked, mock uncertainty on his face.

Paris lifted him an inch, deciding. "I'd say a couple of pounds, maybe."

Lunis sucked in a breath as if that was too much. "I don't know."

"It's fine," Sophia said with a sigh. "How about your equipment? I'm sure you'll have some, right? To shut down the signal on the satellite."

Paris nodded. "About that. Do you think you can help us get hold of a laptop? The one that Faraday built is too big and a total fire hazard."

"You built a computer?" Sophia asked, impressed. "You are a smart squirrel."

"I built a fort last week, and you didn't compliment me," Lunis seethed.

Sophia rolled her eyes. "It was out of pillows, and you got feathers everywhere when you blew on it."

The blue dragon shrugged. "I was testing its strength. It appears that if I were the fourth little piggy, the big bad wolf would have gotten me. I'd be smoked bacon…" He looked off dreamily. "Mmmmm, can we get some bacon?"

Sophia snapped. "Focus, Lun. Yes, Paris, we can get you a laptop."

She then turned to face the Rogue Riders. "I want you all to accompany us. We don't know how these drones are armed. You'll protect us while Faraday shuts down the signal. And no phones until this mess is over. Actually, I have half a mind to ban phones permanently."

"Someone sounds like stuffy Hiker Wallace," Lunis teased. "You're getting to be a real stick in the mud in your old age."

"Who is Hiker Wallace?" Paris asked.

"He's the leader of the Dragon Elite," Sophia stated. "I'm his second in command and the tactical field leader." She whipped around to face her dragon. "And I'm not a stick in the mud. Which reminds me, would you stop tracking mud through the mansion?"

He shrugged. "I'll try but making mud cakes is a messy business."

Faraday regarded the dragon with complete awe. "Brilliant. This is going to be so enlightening, studying dragons."

"Don't count on it," Sophia muttered. "If you want some bad jokes, then it will be a great time, but there probably won't be much enlightenment."

Paris laughed, knowing that Faraday was in good hands. She set him on the grass. "I hope it's okay that I take my leave now. The squirrel knows the coordinates and pretty much all the details of the plan. I'm only the one to ask the favor and deliver the scientist."

Sophia gave her a look of pride. "That's crucial in this fight for justice."

Paris smiled. "Well, I'd stay, but I have another friend who needs my help tonight, and the planetary alignment is tomorrow, so my schedule is quite full."

"Tell me about it," Lunis related. "I'm so busy lately that I haven't had time to feed my pet rock."

Sophia groaned. "Please don't."

Lunis giggled. "It's probably stone-cold dead..."

CHAPTER THIRTY-ONE

The passionflower was even more beautiful than Paris remembered. Or maybe it was the way Hemingway had framed it in the memorial shrine that made it look extra enchanting.

She had to admit that there did seem to be a special art form to flower arranging that capitalized on beauty, drawing out the unique shapes, sizes, and colors of plants.

The greenhouse on the Enchanted Grounds was empty save for Hemingway, Paris, and the flowers. Hemingway seemed to be in a meditative state as he slid a stalk of greenery into place, choosing a deliberate spot instead of haphazardly sticking it somewhere.

The passionflower was in the center of the organic arrangement that was full of interesting plants. Paris had many questions but didn't want to break his intense concentration. She had felt like she was trespassing on a special moment. However, when she returned to Happily Ever After College and popped into the greenhouse to find out what time they were going into the Bewilder Forest, he'd asked her to stay. He'd said it in such a way that it had rendered her speechless—as if he needed her to be there.

The memorial shrine appeared done when Hemingway stepped back, tilting his head to the side to regard it from a different angle.

Paris thought it was incredibly beautiful and represented the many complex emotions that Hemingway must have been experiencing as he reflected on letting go of his mother.

Paris knew that he had never known the woman who gave birth to him. She wasn't the ghost who haunted the Bewilder Forest. She was a memory of the woman who had drowned herself in Mirror Lake after giving birth to Hemingway. Ghosts, Paris had learned, weren't entirely real. They seemed to be because they could speak and move and could harness energy and move things, hurt people, or affect electricity, nature, or animals.

However, they were more like shadows than beings. Ghosts were very much like the shadow that a living person cast before they died. Their ghosts resembled them in appearance somewhat, they moved like them, but they were hollow and chained to the Earth until released.

Shaking his head, Hemingway swiped his hand through the air, making all of the plants in the arrangement fly out of their spots and drop onto the workstation where they'd started. The passion flower was the only thing that remained, sticking straight up in the air from the green florist foam.

"Why did you do that?" Paris asked in shock, finally breaking the silence. "It looked beautiful."

Again, Hemingway shook his head. "The first draft of anything is shit."

She recognized the words as belonging to the "famous" Hemingway, as the grounds keeper would often refer to the writer.

"Well, I'm sure the next attempt will be perfect," Paris consoled.

"I don't think so," Hemingway stated, chewing on his lip, regarding the plants lying lifeless on the workstation. He looked like he was trying to put together a puzzle—deciding which piece to start with.

Paris held out her hand and placed it on his shoulder, capturing his attention. A look of surprise graced Hemingway's face as he glanced up at her. "Remember what you said that Alice Walker wrote?"

He nodded. "In nature, nothing is perfect, and everything is perfect."

"So you don't have to worry about making the memorial shrine perfect," Paris offered. "As you had also said, let the flowers tell you where they should go, and it will be exactly what you want."

He didn't appear convinced, still chewing on his lip. "I want it to symbolize...her."

"Well, then tell me what you know about your mother," Paris replied.

Hemingway drew in a breath. "According to the fairy godmothers, she was a real romantic—throwing herself into her relationships, falling head over feet for men."

That sounded about right to Paris based on the fact that his mother drowned herself because Hemingway's father had rejected her. She also sounded a bit looney, but she was keeping that to herself.

"She loved literature," Hemingway continued. "Hence my name, the only thing that she gave me. I think that she loved many things, but sadly, she loved things that weren't good for her—passion can go two ways."

Paris considered this idea. Someone could be in love with goodness, or they could be in love with hating things. It was all a choice about how to direct their energy.

After a long bout of silence, Hemingway shrugged. "That's all I really know. Oh, and her name was Mary Noble. I never left Happily Ever After College to research her life or find my other family. It got so easy to stay here, and the fairy godmothers were so good to me. I never wanted to leave here, but now I think I didn't want to leave her...not until now."

"You want to let her go," Paris guessed.

He nodded. "But that's so I can leave here. I think the time is drawing near."

Paris' heart suddenly skipped a beat. "You mean you'd go on a vacation outside of Happily Ever After College?"

"More like take a leave of absence," he stated, his focus back on the passionflower. "If my time with you recently has taught me anything, it's that there's this whole world outside of this bubble where I've lived, and it's overdue that I discover it."

Paris felt annoyed that she'd taken Hemingway to Roya Lane or introduced him to the world outside of Happily Ever After College. That also felt wrong. She should want the best for her friend, and if that was leaving the fairy godmothers, she needed to support him.

"But first, I have to let Mary go," Hemingway said with conviction.

"Then you'll leave here?" Paris asked, unable to keep the disappointment out of her voice.

"Then I'll start thinking about it," Hemingway stated. "It won't be easy, but pretending to be a fairy to stay here is constant stress on my shoulders. The FGA agents are growing more skeptical about the college. It's only a matter of time before my truth reveals itself. Then I'll be kicked out of here. I'd rather do it on my terms."

Paris could understand that—even if she couldn't understand Hemingway wanting to leave the place she'd fallen in love with. However, she was going to force herself to support him in this. She mustered a smile. "Okay, then we need to make this memorial shrine right so you can proceed to the next phase that's right for you." She picked up a flower and held it out to him. "Maybe this time, I can help you put it together."

He offered her a tender look and took the flower. "I'd like that. I think then it will be perfect."

CHAPTER THIRTY-TWO

"So Paris could have put a glamour on me, hiding me from view when we walked through Beverly Hills," Faraday said while hurrying down a busy street in West Hollywood.

Sophia shrugged. "It's not easy pulling off a selective disguising spell that makes it so that I can see you and Lunis but others can't. Disguises happen to be one of my specialties and putting them on Lunis has given me a lot of practice. Paris maybe couldn't pull it off."

"Or maybe she wanted to stuff you in a duffle bag," Lunis offered, not only disguised so others on the road didn't see him as a dragon but also under a compartment spell so that he didn't take up the entire sidewalk.

"Well, maybe you can teach Paris how to do this selective disguising spell so that I don't have to ride around in a duffle bag," Faraday raced to keep up with the dragon and rider, who moved gracefully and in a nice rhythm with each other.

"So you can't do any magic, even though you were once a magician?" Sophia asked curiously.

He shook his head. "No, not since becoming trapped as a squirrel. But I wasn't ever good with magic—"

"Hence the whole getting stuck as a squirrel," Lunis cut in.

Faraday sighed. "Well, it was a tricky set of spells and involving time travel complicated things. But truthfully, I've always been better at science than magic. Now magitech is being understood better, and that's where I excel."

"Then you'll like my sister, Liv," Sophia offered as they rounded a corner. "And you'll like where I'm taking you."

"To get a computer?" Faraday asked, intrigued.

Sophia nodded proudly. "It's John's electronic repair shop."

"So it's a refurbished laptop, then?" Faraday questioned.

Sophia shook her head. "Although the shop has been closed for fifteen years, Alicia, a magitech scientist who married my brother Clark although she was in love with John, has been keeping her projects going there."

"Wow, things are so complicated in the Beaufont world," Faraday remarked, having heard this history from Paris but still surprised by it.

"So true," Lunis stated. "The Beaufonts are drama with a capital D."

"We aren't either," Sophia argued. "It's just that we've had to do certain things to protect our family and places in the House of Fourteen."

"I think the Beaufonts go to greater lengths to protect each other than most," Faraday observed.

"I think you're right," Sophia said tenderly. "Anyway, before, the electronic repair shop specialized in fixing toasters and microwaves. However, over time, John and Alicia started dabbling more in magitech with Liv assisting them when she wasn't working on House business or doing something for Papa Creola. If anyone has a laptop that's up to your specs with more bells and whistles than you antici-pated, it will be Alicia."

"I can't wait," Faraday said enthusiastically.

"So you gave up going back to being a real man to stay in this timeline with Paris?" Lunis questioned.

Faraday nodded. "It was a no-brainer. I mean, she's Paris and my best friend. Being around you two is another reason for sticking around. I didn't get to hang out with dragons and riders in my old life.

Or study at fairy godmother college. Or have the opportunity to fix global problems that make a big difference."

Lunis grinned. "Being able to hang out with me is pretty much worth giving up being human."

"You can shrink yourself with a compartment spell," Sophia began. "But I wonder if you can shrink your ego. Otherwise, I don't think all of us will fit in the electronics repair shop with it."

Faraday laughed, enjoying the dragon's and rider's constant banter. "Being in the presence of a dragon is very surreal and fascinating. The Beaufonts seem to be connected to everyone too, knowing Mother Nature and Father Time and Bermuda Laurens and King Rudolf Sweetwater."

"The last one is more of a curse that I think plagues the Beaufonts," Lunis joked. "No matter what, that parasitic fae won't go away."

Sophia paused in front of a boarded-up shop with a faded sign that read John's Electronic Shop. She gave Faraday a look of excitement. "Are you ready to meet another magitech scientist and someone who made significant strides in the field?"

"Am I?" he answered, his eyes wide. "The only way this day could get better is if I got to ride a dragon."

She winked at him. "Then it sounds like it's your lucky day!"

CHAPTER THIRTY-THREE

"I think it's perfect." Hemingway stepped back and admired the memorial shrine that he and Paris had put together.

"It truly is," she agreed, having enjoyed the art form of flower arranging. Hemingway's passion definitely inspired it. She liked watching him work. He got this intense look on his rugged face when he was thinking, and it somehow made him more attractive. There were so many sides to Hemingway, and it surprised Paris how much she enjoyed learning about them.

Hemingway turned his gaze to Paris. "Thanks for your help."

Blushing, Paris looked out the greenhouse glass at the Enchanted Grounds. The golden light of the setting sun was making the lawn glow and shimmer like a green sea. "Do you want to take the shrine now or wait until after sunset?"

"Now," he answered, copying her movement and looking out toward the Bewilder Forest, which was growing darker.

"Okay, well, I can wait here until you finish," Paris replied. "I can fetch Mae Ling and bring her to the edge of the forest for when you're ready."

Hemingway shook his head and reached for her hand. "I'd like you to come with me to place the memorial shrine if you're willing."

"Of course," Paris said, surprised by the invite and his hand in hers —it was warm and strong. "I didn't want to interfere with your special moment."

"You being there is what will make it special," Hemingway argued. "I wouldn't even be doing this if it wasn't for you. Watching the things you've had to deal with has inspired me. You could have stayed stuck at Roya Lane. You could have avoided the Deathly Shadow and not rescued your parents. But you keep pushing yourself to evolve and face your fears."

He regarded the swaying trees in the distance with a speculative expression. "I don't think that we progress unless we conquer the things that scare us. Letting her go has scared me in the past, but her being here isn't good for her, me, or the college. It's time that I let her go, and I want you to be as much a part of that as you're willing to."

Paris squeezed his hand. "I'm honored and will be by your side for all of it."

"Thank you." Hemingway looked at her again. "That will make it easier, although I hope that exorcising the ghost of my mother from the college will be easy enough."

"It won't be easy or straightforward," Mae Ling said from the door, having entered soundlessly with a serious expression.

CHAPTER THIRTY-FOUR

"What?" Shock covered Hemingway's face. "Getting rid of my mother's ghost will be complicated? How much so?"

Mae Ling strode through the green house, appraising the many interesting plants as she passed. When she arrived in front of the pair, she regarded them thoughtfully. "When a person's ghost stays on Earth, it's because they have unresolved issues. They've tethered themselves to a place because they're unwilling to move on. Your mother will fight to stay—clinging onto her grievances and regrets."

"How can we help you?" Paris knew that it was Mae Ling who knew the spell for exorcising the ghost.

"Hemingway has done a lot of the work by getting to this point," Mae Ling explained. "Although your mother haunting the Bewilder Forest at night has meant it was off-limits to most, we couldn't force the ghost out without your permission. If there is one person who wants a ghost to stay, that's enough to keep them in place."

"Wow, that's interesting," Paris mused.

"So the fact that I want her gone helps?" Hemingway questioned.

"Yes," Mae Ling confirmed. "Therefore it's important that you let her go without any hesitation before we start the spell. Then you'll have to remain clear-headed. That's what I'll need from you."

"I can do that," Hemingway said with conviction.

"She won't make it easy though," Mae Ling warned. "Your mother's ghost will try and convince you to hold on to her. For Mary, she's clinging onto you now because she regrets abandoning you all those years ago."

"Oh," Hemingway said, remorse in his voice.

"So no matter what she says or does, you have to stay impassive to her," Mae Ling explained.

Hemingway gulped, not looking as confident as before.

Realizing that his hand was still in hers, Paris squeezed it, offering silent reassurance.

Mae Ling's eyes swiveled down to their intertwined hands before looking directly at Paris. "From you, I'll need something very important that only you can offer."

Paris blinked, waiting for Mae Ling to continue.

"Your demon blood will make this exorcism somewhat more reliable," Mae Ling stated. "When the time comes, you'll need to offer it to me."

"When is that?" Paris questioned.

"You'll know," Mae Ling answered.

Paris didn't at all like that answer. "How am I supposed to do that?"

To her surprise, Mae Ling removed a small pocket knife from her jacket and held it out to Paris.

Paris' eyes widened with horror, but it was Hemingway who bolted forward, shaking his hands. "No, I've changed my mind. I'm not going to have Paris cut herself."

"The demon blood is one of the most reliable ways to seal the ghost away," Mae Ling stated. "I'll use quite a lot of power to exorcise the spirit and send her from the Bewilder Forest. But without something like demon blood, she can come back, and spirits often do, making exorcism unreliable. With Paris, you have a better chance of this working and lasting."

"It's fine, Hemingway." Paris offered him a reassuring look. "I want to do it."

"But you'll have to cut yourself," he argued.

"It's a small laceration," she countered. "I do that all the time while gardening. At least this time, it will serve a purpose. And I like the idea that my demon blood serves a purpose for good."

"Paris, you don't have to do this."

"I want to," she stated with confidence. "Please let me do this for you."

He drew in a breath and closed his eyes for half a beat. When he opened them, he didn't look as encouraged about this whole thing as before, but he still nodded. "Okay, fine. But only a small cut and be careful."

Paris took the knife and slipped it into her pocket, grateful that she could help him, and that oddly enough, it was her demon blood that would do it.

CHAPTER THIRTY-FIVE

When Sophia, Lunis, and Faraday entered the dark electronics repair shop, a couple was standing in the middle of the dusty store. They wore tense expressions as they ran their eyes over the magician, then the compacted dragon, and finally Faraday.

"I got your message," the woman said in a thick Italian accent. She had long thick brown hair and looked worried.

"Ironic that Soph texted you a message on your phone to tell you not to use your phone, huh?" Lunis teased.

The dragonrider rolled her eyes. "I had to tell Alicia and Clark to meet us here so they could help Faraday with a computer."

Alicia pointed at the squirrel. "You're the scientist Sophia told us about?"

He nodded, nervously fidgeting with his paws. Faraday had never been good with meeting new people. Really, he had never been good with people—not until Paris.

"He can talk," Lunis said in a rush.

"Not that you let him much," Sophia added.

"Well, nice to meet you, Faraday. I'm Alicia, a magitech scientist and this is Clark, a Councilor for the House of Fourteen. He's been able to communicate with several authorities to alert them to the problem with the phones. It appears that your solution is the only viable one, so I'm grateful that you're on the case."

If Faraday could blush, he'd be bright red. He didn't know what to say, so he gulped and nodded again.

"Alicia was once a chicken," Lunis offered. "So she knows all about having a tiny brain but still being smart."

"Isn't there an episode of Pokémon you should be watching?" Sophia asked her dragon.

"I couldn't talk when I was a chicken though," Alicia related thoughtfully. "Actually, it's fascinating—your story. Sophia filled me in. I hope that's okay."

Faraday nodded again, his teeth chattering with nervousness. It was being in the presence of such important people along with the pressure that he'd put on himself, taking this major case. All of a sudden, he realized what he'd gotten himself into.

Alicia smiled politely. "Well, I have some computers for you to check out, depending on what you need. They're right over here." She held out her hand to a workstation lined with shiny, sleek laptops.

Faraday felt ridiculous when he nodded yet again.

"You want me to stick you up there, little guy?" Lunis leaned down and eyed Faraday as though he might be ill or have lost his voice. "It's really high."

Thankfully this question gave Faraday the opportunity for a different response. This time, he shook his head and scampered across the floor, climbing up a stool and hopping onto the workstation. Checking out the computers—fueled with magitech—gave him the much-needed task that hopefully would make his nervousness go away.

Alicia, Clark, and Sophia all exchanged tentative looks as the squirrel went to work, tapping on the various laptops, checking out their specs.

"So, did either of you catch the sports game last night?" Lunis asked in a nervous sing-song.

"Which sports game?" Clark asked curiously.

"I don't know," Lunis answered. "Just trying to ease the tension created by the socially awkward scientist squirrel who has offered to save the world but doesn't want to prove my point that he can talk. I sort of want to eat him because of it."

Faraday looked up suddenly, his eyes wide with horror.

"No eating Paris' squirrel," Sophia stated with authority before giving Faraday a commiserating look. "Don't worry, Lunis is all talk… like, the dragon never shuts up."

Alicia let out a forced laugh. "We won't bother you, Faraday, while you check out the devices, but please let me know if you have questions."

"Speaking of computers," Lunis began, "do any of you know how one of them gets drunk?"

"They don't," Sophia muttered and sighed.

"It takes screenshots!" Lunis busted out with a laugh.

"Oh, wow," Clark said, with an uncomfortable laugh. "I forgot how much you like telling jokes."

"I haven't," Sophia groused. "I wish he liked telling funny jokes."

"They are hilarious," Lunis stated. "I have a whole slew of time travel jokes for when I get to see Liv again."

"Oh, classy," Sophia said darkly. "I haven't seen my sister in fifteen years, and you're going to inundate her with bad jokes that point out the fact that she got lost in another dimension and missed out on over a decade of our lives."

"Too soon, huh?" Lunis said mock-seriously. "I can wait…"

"That might be in order," Clark agreed rather seriously.

"Okay, I've waited. How about now?" the blue dragon joked.

Faraday resisted the urge to laugh, thinking that it might come off as rude, although he sensed that Lunis' antics—which were constant—amused Sophia.

"Speaking of Liv," Sophia began. "Have either of you heard from Papa Creola yet?"

Both Alicia and Clark shook their heads, disappointment heavy in their eyes.

"Yeah, me neither." Sophia sighed. "I hope he allows us to see her soon. Paris said that Liv had seen her, Plato, and John, so we have to be next."

"John saw her?" Alicia asked with a hiccup of surprise.

Sophia nodded. "Yeah, apparently."

"I wonder how he is." Alicia seemed to be mostly talking to herself.

"When I saw him recently, he was the same as always," Sophia offered. "Happy and sweet."

Faraday caught a look of regret flicker in the magitech scientist's eyes. He knew from Paris that Alicia and John had once been together, but when Liv and Stefan went missing, they separated. Alicia needed to reserve Liv's position in the House of Fourteen so she married Clark. John needed to keep Paris safe so he became a detective for FLEA after faking being a fairy.

"Well, I hope we're next to see them," Clark stated. "It's so difficult knowing that they're back, but we're unable to visit."

Sophia nodded. "It's painful, but time travel does a number on people's psyche, according to Papa Creola. He's not taking any risks. And you know how much he favors Liv. There's no way he's taking a chance with her going crazy when we just got her back."

"I wanted to make a joke about time travel here," Lunis sounded annoyed. "But you all didn't like it."

A squeak of laughter popped out of Faraday's mouth against his permission, making everyone look at him suddenly. He busied himself again, checking out the computers, trying to pretend he hadn't been listening.

"I'm currently looking to hire teenagers with expertise in time travel," Lunis stated.

"No, you're not," Sophia argued.

"Yeah, I am. Twenty plus years of experience required." The dragon laughed.

Thankfully so did Alicia and Clark, covering up the fact that Faraday did too.

"Do you think that one of those laptops will work for you?" Alicia smiled at the squirrel.

He nodded.

"Oh, good," Alicia stated. "I picked out lighter options since I know that Lunis will have to carry it."

"I'm a dragon," Lunis stated dryly. "I've carried Sophia after she dined at an Indian buffet. I think I can handle her, a squirrel, and a laptop."

"Anyone you know who is in the market for a dragon?" Sophia asked the couple. "He eats way too much sugar, plays video games really loudly, and chews with his mouth open."

"He sounds lovely," Lunis replied. "I'll take him."

Sophia's phone buzzed in her pocket. She gave the others a tentative look. "I think I have to get that."

"But the phones are addictive," Alicia argued.

"Yeah, but I had my phone on silent, which means…"

"That it's probably Father Time," Clark supplied.

"Exactly." Sophia retrieved her phone from her pocket and laughed. "Yeah, it's Papa Creola, all right."

"Did he ask about me?" Lunis craned his neck to read her phone.

She shook her head. "No, he says that as soon as Faraday picks out a laptop, he has news for us."

All eyes swiveled up to stare at Faraday. He stiffened, definitely feeling the pressure. Quickly, he pointed at the closest laptop. "That one. That's the one I'd like. Please and thank you."

"See!" Lunis exclaimed. "I told you he could talk."

"Very impressive." Alicia smiled. "Good choice."

Sophia's phone dinged again. She glanced at it.

"What does he say?" Clark asked in a rush.

"He says that Faraday should start the software updates right away for the program he created to stop the signal," Sophia read before looking up. "They'll take a lot of time."

"Well, Papa Creola would know," Lunis muttered, stretching to a lying position on the floor, suddenly looking tired.

Her phone buzzed again. "Mama Jamba wants the phones fixed as soon as possible. Love is at an all-time low."

"Okay, I'll get straight to installing." Faraday tapped on the keys with his paws.

"Do you need my help?" Alicia asked.

Sophia's phone buzzed once more. Her head jerked up. "We get to see Liv and Stefan!"

CHAPTER THIRTY-SIX

"When?" Clark asked, his face instantly covered in excitement. Sophia was suddenly shaking as she looked at her phone. "Tomorrow mid-morning at ten-twenty-six."

"Can he be more specific?" Lunis teased.

"He'll have a reason for the timing." Clark was nearly stammering.

"It will take until tomorrow afternoon for me to have the software ready," Faraday explained, nervously joining the conversation.

"So we'll go to see Liv and Stefan," Sophia stated. "And when we finish on Roya Lane, we'll head up into the stratosphere to shut down the signal."

Lunis yawned. "Good. That gives me time to nap."

"I can't believe we'll finally get to see them," Sophia said, her shoulders scrunched up to her head with delight.

"All of us?" Alicia asked.

Sophia's phone buzzed. She laughed when she looked at him. "Yes, but Lunis can't come if he tells time travel jokes."

"Well, looks like I'm sitting this one out, guys," Lunis muttered.

Sophia sent him a rude glare. "Are you serious? You can't refrain from telling bad jokes for an hour to see my sister, who has been gone for fifteen years?"

Before he could answer, her phone buzzed again. She sighed and shook her head. "Papa Creola says that it might pain you too much and he wants you to stay with Faraday while he does the installations."

"Good, because I have too many time travel jokes for them to go to waste by me not being able to tell them." Lunis rolled onto his side to get more comfortable.

Sophia's phone dinged. "Yeah, Papa Creola says you can go the next time to see Liv and Stefan. Then your jokes will be less irritating."

Lunis huffed. "Well, speaking of cranky old men, I invented a time travel machine and went back and killed my grandfather to see if I wouldn't be born…It was the worst way to learn that I'm adopted."

The phone buzzed. "Papa Creola says you should be grateful that Mama Jamba has your back, Lunis. Otherwise, you'd be erased."

"Hey, tell Papa Creola that he should start a time travel school." Lunis snickered. "Classes begin last Tuesday."

Sophia groaned. "Is that the last one?"

Another *ding* on her phone stole her attention. She sighed. "Apparently not."

"Well, if the father of time says I haven't finished, then how could I be," Lunis joked. "He's a great guy. He's my favorite time-traveling friend. We go back years."

No one was surprised to hear Sophia's phone *ding*. She let out a breath of relief. "Oh, good. That was the last one."

"Yeah, all this entertaining has tuckered me out." Lunis yawned, laid his head down, and shut his eyes at once. "I'll work on some more material for later."

"My apologies in advance, Faraday." Sophia shook her head.

The squirrel grinned. "It's fine. I like the jokes because I used to be addicted to time travel, but that's all in the past now."

Lunis awoke with a start, howling with laughter. "Oh, the squirrel and I are going to be great friends. I can already tell."

CHAPTER THIRTY-SEVEN

The gravity of the moment didn't really register for Paris until Hemingway and she made their way to the edge of the Bewilder Forest. He was carrying the large memorial shrine. It was the perfect size, not too big but enough that its symbolism was powerful. In his strong hands, it was secure as he took great care not to damage any of the flowers. Just before leaving the greenhouse, he'd placed a preserving spell on the bouquet. It would never wilt or die for as long as he kept renewing the spell.

"I'll wait here until you're ready for me," Mae Ling said when they reached the forest.

Hemingway nodded to her over his shoulder before giving Paris a tentative look that seemed to say, "You're still coming, right?"

She offered him a thoughtful look as she hurried to take a place beside him in answer to his silent question.

The cold of the forest covered Paris as soon as they entered. Although the temperature was always the same at Happily Ever After College, the Bewilder Forest was different thanks to the ghost of Hemingway's mother. She would come out as soon as the sun set completely. Still, the chill she brought with her seemed to be a precursor to her arrival.

Pulling her leather jacket tighter around her, Paris tried to cover the fact that she was cold. She didn't want Hemingway worried about her right then…or ever. She wanted to be there for him that night, not having him concerned for her well-being.

Paris didn't know how far into the Bewilder Forest they'd venture to place the memorial shrine. Hemingway hadn't told her what it would involve or where it would be. He wasn't a man who said a lot or offered too much information. She liked that about him because when he did speak, his words carried great weight. That very much reminded her of Uncle John, who was soft-spoken most of the time but used his words wisely.

"There's a spot where I always know I can find her." Hemingway broke the silence.

Paris nodded. "That's where you're going to place the memorial shrine?"

"I think so," he answered. "It's where I met her for the first time—when I was ten years old. Before that, I'd heard about the ghost of my mother from Willow. She'd warned me not to go into the forest, unsure what would happen to me. However, one night, I awoke with a start and found my bedroom window open, although I remembered closing it."

The sound of twigs and leaves crunching underfoot filled the air between them for a moment before Hemingway continued. "The moon was full that night and made the Enchanted Grounds so bright. For some reason, the light made the prospect of entering a dark forest not so scary…not like it had before. So I climbed out my window and scaled down to the first floor. I remember running for the forest, thinking that if I got caught, they'd send me to an orphanage in the real world. Even then, I knew what a gift it was being raised by loving fairy godmothers and my identity preserved instead of being turned over to the authorities. My father didn't want me, so I'd be an orphan."

Paris was surprised by all the words Hemingway was suddenly sharing with her. It was nice to hear him speak, but it felt better to know he was sharing something of great importance with her. Better still was the realization that he needed her there for this "letting go" part of the ceremony. He wanted her there. To cap it all off, when it was time to seal the ghost of his mother away, Paris' demon blood would serve a purpose above and beyond making her repelled by evil and led to fight it.

"I was astonished when I got to the Bewilder Forest to find Willow and Mae Ling standing, waiting for me," Hemingway went on. "They told me that it was time for me to meet the ghost of my mother and that they didn't believe she would harm me...but only me."

Paris gasped with surprise. "So they had led you there, then? Those tricky fairies."

He nodded with a slight grin. "I don't know how many nights they waited out by the trees waiting for me to sneak out to the Bewilder Forest, but thinking back, I believe they were waiting for me to be ready—meaning brave enough to venture out on my own, rather than to have their encouragement. There was something to it. If they had told me to go into the forest to meet my mother, I would have done it before I was ready. When I did enter the Bewilder Forest, I wasn't the least bit scared by her appearance or strangeness. Over time, I figured out that she minded me and therefore, I could protect those she threatened."

Paris remembered when she'd first met the ghost of Hemingway's mother. She tried to do everything she could to harm Paris, but Hemingway came to her rescue, calling the spirit off.

"For a while," Hemingway continued, "I visited her every night, believing I was spending time with my mother...wishing it could be her. Then one day, I realized that she was only a projection of someone who had been gone for a very long time. It was that day that I finally understood that my mother was forever gone and there was no getting her back. However, it took me until now to know that letting her go is as much for her as it is for me. A soul can't be free as long as its ghost haunts the Earth. A person can't move on, as long as they hold onto something that's gone."

"I can tell that you've thought your way through all of this," Paris offered. "That couldn't have been easy."

"I felt my way through it," he corrected. "I don't believe that matters of the heart can be understood with the mind, just as we can't process complex thoughts with emotions. The mind and the heart are very different and for unique and separate purposes."

Hemingway was so wise, and it made her wish that he could be a fairy god…father. Or something for FGA even though he wasn't a fairy. The world could benefit from more love crafted by those who were logical and also passionate.

He gracefully approached the babbling brook that snaked over mossy rocks and fallen logs. He set the memorial shrine next to the water, standing back suddenly as though he didn't want to be close to it for long.

"This is where you met the ghost of your mother?" The fading sunlight made it difficult for Paris to make out too many details in the darkening forest.

He nodded.

Paris wanted to say something but again felt like she was trespassing on a moment, even if Hemingway wanted her there for it.

"Mother," he began, "I know the events of your life broke you. I can't regret the way things happened because it won't do me any good since this was the life I was given. You took your life because you couldn't stand the pain. All these years, I've tried to understand it. My lesson has been in learning from your weaknesses. You took your life because the world broke you, but I won't let that be my story. As the famous Hemingway said, 'The world breaks everyone, and afterward, many are strong at the broken places.'"

He took a step backward and shook his head with a sober look in his eyes. He pressed his hands together as though in prayer, holding them calmly to his chest. "Goodbye, Mary. I hope that somehow, some way, you find peace out there in the ether. And I hope that in your absence, I do as well."

Hemingway lowered his hands, the one closest to Paris catching her fingers—gripping them tenderly. He glanced sideways at her, the waning sunlight illuminating the side of his face. To her surprise, she didn't see him as broken at all. If anything, more than usual, Hemingway seemed whole, as if letting his mother go was how he put himself back together.

142

The walk back through the Bewilder Forest to where they'd started felt shorter. Maybe it was Hemingway who seemed to walk lighter. Or perhaps it was because the sun was quickly setting at that point and Paris knew that the ghost they'd said goodbye to would be coming out soon—challenging them, not wanting to be ousted from the place she was haunting.

Mary, the ghost of Hemingway's mother, was like a bad house guest at this point. She'd been politely dismissed but was going to lurk around until forcefully asked to leave.

Hemingway didn't say another word for the entirety of the walk, but he kept his fingers intertwined with hers. Strangely, it felt like he was lending her more comfort than the other way around.

When they came to the edge of the Bewilder Forest, the outline of Mae Ling's form was visible in the faint sunlight, which was quickly disappearing. She waited until they'd stepped through the line of trees before she offered Hemingway a sympathetic look and bowed her head.

"What you've done isn't easy," the fairy godmother said to him. "But you're doing it with the right spirit in your heart and sentiment in your mind. Are you ready to finish what you started?"

Hemingway released Paris' hand and stepped forward deliberately. "Yes, and I want to thank you for all the support you've offered me from the beginning. You and Willow have protected me from the beginning, sheltered me when that's what I needed, and now you're here to help with this."

Mae Ling nodded. "Helping you has always been a joy. Don't think I've done it for any other reason. I've seen you every day that you've lived, and on all of them, you've smiled. A person like that is one who fairy godmothers are supposed to serve."

"Well, thank you." Hemingway spun back to face the darkening forest. "I'm ready to go if you are."

Paris nodded and turned to face the same direction.

Mae Ling stepped up next to Hemingway on the other side. "You're the one who has to be the most ready. If you are, then our jobs are too."

CHAPTER THIRTY-NINE

In a matter of seconds, it seemed that the sun had gone to sleep and the darkness had taken over the Bewilder Forest, giving it that eerie feeling that Paris had felt so often when exploring it. The twinkling flowers sparkled to life almost immediately once they were a short way into the trees, almost as if they sensed the ominous task ahead and wanted to lend their light.

The three stepped through the plants and made their way to the path, careful to avoid things like the bewitched vines. Paris was less afraid of them with Mae Ling with them. She hadn't worried much when it was her and Hemingway before in the darkened Bewilder Forest, and less so with the fairy godmother. There was something about Mae Ling that made one feel safe and as if nothing could harm them as long as she was there to help.

"So what do we do?" Paris whispered, feeling it had to be said.

"We walk on and wait," Mae Ling answered, not at all sounding put out by the seemingly stupid question.

Obviously, they were looking for the ghost who haunted the Bewilder Forest, but it felt to Paris that they should arm themselves somehow, knowing that there would be conflict. Mary, the spirit, wouldn't want to leave. The other two times Paris had seen her, she'd been raging mad. It felt like they should be on guard somehow, but if Mae Ling said they walked and waited, then that's what she would do.

Ten minutes later, they'd moved deeper into the woods, accompanied by the twinkling lights and the sound of nocturnal animals. Occasional openings in the foliage overhead showed the purple sky. The forest at night was rather peaceful, although full of strange creatures and plants. However, Paris longed for the idea that soon it would be accessible to others since the ghost wouldn't haunt it during the twilight hours.

Mae Ling paused suddenly, her arms outstretched, halting Paris and Hemingway on either side of her. "She's here," the fairy godmother said in a hushed voice.

Paris tensed. She noticed Hemingway do the same.

Mae Ling looked at him. "Remember, no matter what, you have to keep your intention clear. If you change your mind, that changes everything, and I can't help you let her go. Only you can do that."

He nodded, an adamant look on his face.

Mae Ling turned to peer at Paris. "Stay strong, child. When the time comes, you know what needs to happen."

Paris nodded, but the truth was she didn't know. She didn't know when this magical time was that Mae Ling had been very vague about. Although Paris knew she had to spill her blood, she didn't know where or how and was worried that she'd screw it all up. But there was no time for questions because a moment later a piercing howl filled the night air, sending a chill down Paris' back.

CHAPTER FORTY

The ghost arrived with an icy wind that swept Paris' hair back and instantly made her cold all over. Leaves and debris hit the trio in the face as the gust rocked the trees.

Like before, the Lady of the Lake flew through the air, soaring straight for them. Although Paris knew that Hemingway could control her to an extent, that didn't keep the fear from pulsing in her veins. He could control her before, but when the ghost learned they were there to get rid of her, would she be so compliant with his orders? Her instinct said, "no."

Swallowing down the gripping fear, Paris recognized the transparent figure with long dark hair in the white gown. A painful shiver ran down Paris' back as she looked at the hollow sockets for the spirit's eyes. Water droplets fell from the end of the ghost's nightgown, but they didn't gather on the ground. Like the Lady of the Lake, the water was there and not. It was a projection, but that didn't mean the ghost didn't have power, as evidenced by the howl that pierced Paris' ears.

The chill that cut through the air made Paris' teeth chatter, suddenly unbelievably cold to the bone. Beside her, Hemingway lifted his hand as though silently trying to halt the ghost of his mother before she soared right through them. Thankfully it worked, and the apparition halted a few yards away, swaying creepily before them.

The Lady of the Lake pointed at Paris. "You did this!" the ghost said in a chilly voice that sounded both hoarse and sharp at the same time. "You stole him away, and you're going to pay."

That's what she'd said before. It appeared she was on repeat, reliving the trauma from when Hemingway's father left her when she was pregnant.

Paris sucked in a breath, thinking that her lungs would freeze from the inhale of cold air.

The Lady of the Lake zoomed a few feet closer, her hand still outstretched. "It was you!" the ghost screamed, not giving Paris much space.

Hemingway stepped in between the two. "It wasn't her. Move back."

Paris didn't know if he was talking to her or the ghost of his mother. She decided it wouldn't hurt to put some space between her and the crazy ghost. That's when she noticed that Mae Ling was mouthing a spell, her fingers working silently in front of her. Paris didn't recognize the magic, but apparently, the ghost did.

"Stop it!" Mary yelled, her voice a hoarse growl that filled Paris with horror.

"No, Mother," Hemingway argued, holding out his arm protectively to shield Mae Ling. "It's time you must go. It's time I let you go!"

"You can't!" the ghost exclaimed.

Wind spiraled around them, creating a cyclone of plants and leaves. The twinkling flowers all bowed around them as if they were surrendering to the ghost' power. The force of the wind was making it difficult to stand. Thankfully it didn't deter Mae Ling from whispering the spell. Hemingway glanced back at Paris, checking on her. That gave the Lady of the Lake the opportunity she must have been looking for.

She shot forward, putting her translucent hands around Mae

Ling's throat. Paris thought they'd pass through the small fairy godmother, but an invisible force hauled her off her feet and threw her back several yards, knocking her into a tree trunk and sending her to the forest floor in a heap.

CHAPTER FORTY-ONE

"Mae Ling!" Paris yelled, running to help the fallen woman.

"You can't stop this!" Hemingway exclaimed, still facing his mother. The wind beat at his clothes and hair, but he remained standing firm.

Thankfully, Mae Ling was already rising to her feet when Paris went to help her up. Even more impressive was that she was still muttering the spell. As soon as she was upright, her fingers went back to work.

"You can't let me go," the Lady of the Lake cried. Her voice was no longer a scream but rather a pitiful plea. It hit Paris' heart, making her suddenly sympathize with the ghost chained to the Bewilder Forest. She could only imagine how the sobs falling from his mother's mouth made Hemingway feel.

"Son, you can't get rid of me," Mary wailed. "I'm your mother, and you're all I have left."

Paris wanted to tell him to be strong. To remember why he was doing this and keep any doubt out of his heart. But she knew this was something Hemingway had to do on his own.

To her relief, he pulled his shoulders back and shook his head. "It's time you move on. You don't belong here anymore. I don't want you haunting the forest."

The mournful expression on the ghost's face disappeared at once, replaced by hostile vengeance. "How dare you! I've protected you! I gave birth to you!"

Before, the wind had flattened plants. Now it was knocking down trees, whipping so much around that it was hard to see the sights around them. Mae Ling had reclaimed her position behind Hemingway. Paris stood on the other side of him, wondering how she could help—but it wasn't her time yet. Mae Ling had to contain the ghost and send her away. Then it would be Paris' turn, but she didn't know if there would be any more of the Bewilder Forest left.

"You abandoned me!" Hemingway screamed, his words hardly audible over the howling wind and sounds of breaking branches.

"He abandoned us!" the Lady of the Lake fired back.

A tree beside them cracked as though hit by an invisible ax and fell to the forest floor with a crash, shaking the ground.

"It's time you leave here—my home," Hemingway said, his voice calm once more although hard to hear over the chaos ensuing all around them from the destructive ghost.

"I won't!" Mary yelled and threw out her hands, sending a visible force flecked with red through the air. It hit all three of them, sending them flying like she had done to Mae Ling before. Everything that the force hit toppled to the ground, instantly making the area of the forest around them look like it had been clear cut.

Paris hit her head on something hard but didn't feel it. She rolled to her feet at once, looking around for Mae Ling and Hemingway. To her surprise, the woman was already on her feet. Hemingway was the one still lying on the forest floor, a look of horror on his face as he looked at the destruction all around him—pure offense in his eyes.

He jumped straight to his feet and threw his hands up, sending his powerful force through the air, his magic flecked with bright blue. It hit the ghost and knocked her back several yards. "You will go! And you won't ever haunt this place again. Go, Mary! Leave for good."

The scream that filled the air sent a sharp chill down Paris' spine, but she immediately stiffened. The blood-curdling scream hadn't scared her. It had sought to freeze her—to freeze everything in the forest. Spreading out from the Lady of the Lake was thick frost, and it covered everything, rapidly progressing across the plants and fallen trees and Paris and her friends.

She looked down and saw her hands covered in ice, and for a moment, she thought they were doomed. The ghost would win. Then what would happen to the college?

"Leave now," Hemingway said in a chilling tone although frost covered his mouth and his jaw was seemingly frozen.

"I won't!" Mary howled, drawing out the word with conviction.

"You will!" Mae Ling yelled so loudly and forcefully that it shook the earth and made the icicles that had formed on the trees shatter and fall to the ground.

As quickly as she'd appeared and destroyed everything in the Bewilder Forest, the Lady of the Lake vanished in a plume of smoke with a final scream of protest.

The forest was suddenly silent. Paris tried to blink around at her surroundings, her eyelashes covered in ice crystals. She turned to ask Mae Ling if it was her turn to seal the ghost away, but that would have been impossible because the fairy godmother had fainted and was lying in a heap of frost and destruction.

CHAPTER FORTY-TWO

Hemingway's and Paris' eyes connected and she read the fear in his gaze. He thought that she could be dead. Paris couldn't consider that right then. She had to focus. To do what she came there for. She had to finish this.

"Help her," Paris said, her mouth hardly able to move due to the frost.

Hemingway nodded stiffly and broke out of his icy casing by lumbering forward and nearly falling.

The entire forest was white, providing the light since the twinkling flowers were gone. Everything was gone, knocked down by the wind and killed with frost. It pained Paris' heart as she saw clear to the Enchanted Ground and college buildings, which the trees usually obstructed.

The ground rumbled under their feet, and Paris knew she had to get to work. Moving was difficult and took much more effort than she could ever remember. She felt like she was in a dream where she needed to move but stayed stuck in molasses while the villain of that nightmare raced after her, unobstructed.

Paris mustered strength from the bottom of her soul, knowing that she couldn't fail Hemingway and Mae Ling now. The ground continued to quake, nearly throwing her off-balance.

The thin layer of ice that had formed on Paris' clothes cracked and fell away as she moved her arms. With each attempt at moving, it got easier and warmed her blood.

She managed to slide her hand into her pocket and retrieve the pocket knife. The good news was that she was numb all over and didn't think she'd feel the cut.

Opening the blade, Paris held it to the palm of her hand. Her eyes swiveled to meet Hemingway's—regret heavy in his gaze. They both knew she had to do this. The soil rumbling under their feet and what felt like a permanent frost in a place that was always the perfect temperature reminded them that the Lady of the Lake could return unless Paris sealed her away.

Without another moment of hesitation, Paris sliced the blade across her palm, making an incision that was long and deep. She felt the cut even though she was numb but didn't care.

She dropped the blade, folded her fingers in, and pressed them into the laceration. Blood oozed out over her fingertips and hand. She turned her palm down and squeezed again, sending her demon blood to the ground below. It dripped onto the white frost, contrasting boldly.

Smoke issued up from the ground as if it was suddenly on fire under the dirt and debris. Paris worried that she hadn't done something right or that she needed to do more, but then the forest floor went still. That seemed like a good sign to her.

Then, if signs could make her feel better, the best one of all followed. Starting from where she had spilled her blood, the frost receded as though spring had made winter retreat suddenly. Steam rose from the ground, creating a blanket where the ice had been.

A gentle breeze that Paris associated with the warm grounds of Happily Ever After College sent the vapor away. She looked at Hemingway kneeling next to Mae Ling, and relief filled his face. He must have felt it at his core, and it was written in his eyes—the ghost who had haunted the Bewilder Forest was gone...but so was the forest.

CHAPTER FORTY-THREE

Once the steam was gone, it was clear that the Bewilder Forest had suffered greatly. The ground was black as if it had burned. All the plants were wilted and dead. There wasn't a single tree in the vicinity standing. Worse, Paris worried about all the animals and creatures who called the magical forest home. She knew that getting rid of the Lady of the Lake had to happen, but losing the forest to do that felt wrong.

They'd deal with that later, she decided and hurried over to where Mae Ling lay. "Is she..."

Hemingway nodded, sensing the rest of her words. "She's breathing. I think she exhausted herself with the effort. Willow will know. I should get her to the college."

"Are you okay?" Paris looked him over. The frost had left his hair wet and lying on his forehead, but otherwise, he looked unscathed from the battle.

"I'm fine," he said through a breath. His eyes fell to her hand, which she still had closed. "Your palm. Let me wrap it up."

She shook her head, cradling her hand with her other one. "I'm fine. It's more important that we get Mae Ling to safety. Can you carry her?"

In answer, he slipped his hands under the small woman's body and lifted her to his chest as he stood. "Yes. But I'm bandaging you up as soon as we get her to the mansion."

Paris wasn't going to argue with him. Now that the cold and adrenaline had receded, the stinging pain of the cut made her whole hand throb. "Okay, but I'll also take some whiskey if you're pouring."

He nodded with a sigh. "I think that's a good idea. Let's get going."

Hemingway looked around before starting toward the fairy godmother mansion, seen clearly in the distance, unobstructed by the thick forest. Paris knew that Hemingway had to let go of his mother's ghost, but the fact that he had to lose a place he loved so dearly made her heart hurt for him. She didn't like the irony of it.

She hurried to catch up with him, having to leap over fallen trees and branches. "It will grow back. Don't worry."

He didn't look encouraged by her words, easily traversing across the demolished forest while he carried the fairy godmother. "I don't see how."

"Things will look better in the morning." It was dark without the twinkling flowers, but thankfully the light spilling from the buildings on the Enchanted Grounds in the distance gave them enough light to see.

"I guess," he said, regret in his voice.

Blood continued to drip from Paris' hand, marking the forest floor as they progressed to the edge of what used to be the tree line. They walked in silence for a while, the only sound from their footsteps.

Hemingway paused at the edge of the Bewilder Forest. Paris halted and looked him over, worried that he was out of strength and needed to rest. His chest rose and fell several times as if he was trying to catch his breath.

Remorse filled his eyes. "I loved the forest. I'm so sorry it was the price I paid to let her go."

"I know." Paris lifted her hand reflexively but stopped herself before she placed it on his arm, not wanting to cover him in her blood. "But if anyone can bring the forest back, it will be you."

He pressed his lips together tightly, a painful tenderness in his eyes. Hemingway nodded but didn't look convinced. Then without another word, he turned back to the forest to say a final farewell to the place that had died to set him free.

"Oh my God!" he exclaimed with shock. "It can't be real."

CHAPTER FORTY-FOUR

Paris spun to see what Hemingway was talking about and was also instantly astonished. The frostbitten forest they'd walked through was...different. It was growing back *instantly*. Little green seedlings pushed up through the soil and into the air like a plant growing in a time-lapse video. They quickly grew into saplings that seemed ready to become trees soon.

However, the plants were only growing along a straight line. It was the path that they'd come through. Paris gasped when she realized what was making this part of the forest sprout.

She lifted her hand and opened it, looking at her bloody palm.

"It's your blood," Hemingway said in awe, looking between her hand and the new bright green vegetation of the forest. "You're making the forest come back."

There were tears in his words. Paris choked on her tears, finding her throat constricted. "But then it won't be right," she said when she finally found her voice. All she could think was how it was her demon blood that had made the deadly nightshade pop up for the first time in the forest. If her demon blood was bringing it back, would the forest be full of dangerous plants? Maybe it was better for the Bewilder Forest to die than to be full of evil.

"It's your fairy blood that's bringing it back," Mae Ling said, still in Hemingway's arms. Her voice sounded strained, and it appeared to take a great effort to hold up her head. "Your demon blood sealed the ghost away. The fairy blood was necessary to bring the forest back. Your magician blood will make this unlike it's ever been before. It will make it better."

Paris' eyes widened with shock. She was about to ask Mae Ling if she knew that exorcising the ghost would kill the forest, but before she could, the fairy laid her head down and closed her eyes. Paris sensed that the older woman, who seemed to be all-knowing, knew that it had to be Paris who sealed the ghost away for good and brought back the forest.

Hemingway and Paris caught each other's gaze before they looked back at the forest. In a matter of moments, the green had spread out from the line of blood. New growth covered increasing patches of the damaged earth. At this rate, the Bewilder Forest would be green all over by morning. How long it would take for trees to grow, Paris didn't know, but it sounded like this was brand new territory—literally and figuratively.

Hemingway let out a breath of relief and smiled tenderly at Paris. "You did it. I should have known that if anyone could bring back my forest, it would be you."

CHAPTER FORTY-FIVE

The dining hall was a stir of excited whispers when Paris came down the next morning for breakfast. She would need all the coffee in the world to wake her up after only a couple of hours of sleep. Not having Faraday in her room that night had made it more difficult to go to sleep. And, of course, she'd been worried about Mae Ling, although Headmistress Willow had said she'd make a full recovery when she and Hemingway had brought her to her office.

They had explained what had happened and she nodded, always the picture of poise, saying that they expected as much. Paris had questioned her about what the Bewilder Forest would be like and if it would be okay, spawned by her demon, fairy, and magician blood.

Willow had held up a hand to calm her worry and smiled before saying, "It will be what it will be, and it will be wonderful, like you. Thank you for helping to regrow the forest."

Paris was still in shock from all this, but she was hopeful that the forest ignited from her blood would be at least as nice as the Bewilder Forest.

Knowing that she had a full day of tasks ahead of her since that night was the hour of the planetary alignment, she'd forced herself out of bed after only a couple of hours of sleep. She wouldn't be attending classes that day since more pressing matters demanded her attention.

However, she was surprised to find that Hemingway hadn't slept in either after the long night of turmoil and emotions. She'd left him after having a small glass of whiskey where he'd kindheartedly thanked her, saying he felt too weary to express his full gratitude for all that she'd done but that he hoped to do so in the future. Paris didn't know what that meant, but it made her heart flutter in ways she hadn't known before, and she was a bit nervous to understand fully.

"Did you see it?" Christine asked as Paris sat with an extra-large cup of coffee.

She didn't answer, simply looked across the table at Hemingway.

Chef Ash nodded, leaning forward. "As soon as I opened my eyes, I thought the sun must be brighter. Then I sat up and realized the line of trees that normally obstructs the early morning sun was gone. The Bewilder Forest...what's happened to it?"

"I bet that Becky Montgomery's family is against trees and made the headmistress clear cut it," Christine said in a conspiratorial whisper.

"There's new growth already," Penny stated matter-of-factly.

Everyone paused to look at the unassuming student.

She shrugged, stirring her oatmeal. "I went down to investigate it this morning. There's a clear place where new growth is strongest. Some small saplings already look really sturdy. Smaller growth is expanding out from them as if that's their energy source, but it also appears quite hardy. I think that in a day, the forest will be to knee height. In a week, it will be full. And in a month, well, who knows...it won't be the same though."

"Wow, okay, I had no idea that you'd done an investigative dig," Christine joked. "I only wanted to know what happened to the forest to make it disappear in the night. Apparently, it's not safe to sleep around here."

Paris took a long sip of coffee, her eyes intently on Hemingway, who also didn't appear ready to supply an answer for the group.

Thankfully, Headmistress Willow Starr stood at that precise moment, tapping her spoon to her tea cup, gaining everyone's attention.

"If I may interrupt your breakfast briefly," she began in her polite tone. "I have a few announcements to make. Some of you may have noticed that the Bewilder Forest has disappeared, but new seeds have replenished it. Those will be growing over the next several days and weeks so we ask that you leave them be to flourish until they are strong enough."

This produced excited whispers from around the table. Paris kept her eyes on Hemingway, who also didn't seem able to take his eyes off her.

Willow continued, "You might be asking what happened to the Bewilder Forest. Well, as we warned all of you, it's off-limits at night due to dangers beyond our control."

Many gasped or chatted to their neighbor, making a commotion in the dining room. Willow held up her hand to silence the students.

"It was nothing for you to ever worry about," Willow stated. "Merely something better to avoid. But a recent decision to fully return the forest to Happily Ever After College meant that it was cleared and reseeded. Soon you'll have a brand new forest to explore, both during the day and the night."

She pulled her shoulders back proudly with a wide smile as she looked around the room, her eyes briefly connecting with Paris and Hemingway.

"That's so exciting," Christine stated.

"I'd say," Chef Ash offered. "There are certain herbs I can only harvest at night in a forest. This opens up new opportunities."

"So many opportunities," Penny agreed.

"For now," Willow continued, "Please give our new forest time to get stronger. I'll let you know when it's ready for you to explore, but until then, we're excited at Happily Ever After College to mark a new dawn when we can allow you access to more things."

Paris smiled into her coffee cup, conscious that Hemingway was smiling at her. He had started a new chapter of his life, and she was grateful for his freedom and that she'd helped to be a part of it. She hoped that he'd accompany her after breakfast to visit Mae Ling as they talked about the night before.

"Also, one last announcement," Willow went on. "For your safety, cell phones are still not to be used and are to remain confiscated in my office. I do not mind that the squirrel known as Faraday gave you all access to data and messaging. However, we must take the utmost caution until a global problem resolves."

Paris set down her coffee cup, hoping that her squirrel was having luck with his mission and wishing she could communicate with him. Ironically, she couldn't because the only way she could was compromised—and happened to be what he was working on to save love worldwide.

CHAPTER FORTY-SIX

"You can call me Lunis," the blue dragon said when he awoke to Faraday as if they'd just met.

The squirrel looked up from the computer he'd been working on all through the night. He needed some coffee and maybe an everything bagel with cream cheese.

"I have been calling you Lunis," Faraday remarked through a yawn. Well, he hadn't been calling him anything since the dragon had been asleep for the last eight hours, snoring beside him on the floor of the electronics repair shop.

"My boss calls me 'The computer,'" Lunis remarked while stretching, still in his compacted form to fit inside the building.

"You mean Sophia?" Faraday asked, confused.

Lunis shook his head. "Yeah, and they don't call me that because of calculation skills. It's because I go to sleep when left unattended for five minutes."

"Wow, you never stop with the jokes, do you?" Faraday questioned.

"It's a gift to those around me. You're welcome. Do you know that some people go all day without telling a single joke?"

Faraday nodded. "I've met these people."

"Total squares," Lunis said, shaking his tail. "So when will you be done? The boss is gone, and I want powdered sugared donuts. She never lets me have powdered sugar donuts."

"Why not?"

"Because she says afterward I look like a gangster."

"Oh," he said, at first not getting the joke. Then coughed out a long, "Ohhhhhh…"

Lunis laughed. "I mean, I'm sort of a violent guy. I went to Dunkin Donuts and ordered a dozen chocolate cake donuts. The best donuts in the world, I might add. Anyway, the cashier asked if I wanted to box them…they've banned me ever since."

Faraday laughed, wondering how he'd somehow met the best dragon in the world on his first occasion meeting one. Lunis had it all. Jokes, humor, flight, courage. "Hey, I was hoping we could get bagels."

"I don't do bagels," Lunis stated decisively. "I don't make wrong decisions in my life. If you do, this is where we part ways, squirrel."

"Well, maybe this once you can go to the bagel store with me?" Faraday asked. "I can't really order them myself since I'm a talking squirrel and all. You can because you're a dragon and that's a bit more acceptable."

"It is more acceptable, and we're getting donuts," Lunis stated. "You'll learn to like my ways."

Well, the dragon was almost perfect. He didn't compromise, but at least he was funny about it. "Yeah, fine. We can get donuts, but I have to start an update first on the computer. Then it can run while we're gone, and I can finish up when we return."

Faraday gave the dragon a very pointed look.

"What?" Lunis asked after a moment.

"Don't you have a joke?" Faraday questioned. "Something about computers or updates on software or whatever?"

Lunis suddenly looked offended. "You know, I'm not a clown and simply performing on cue nonstop for you people."

"I'm sorry," Faraday said, typing on the computer. "I guess it does get exhausting always having to come up with a joke for all occasions."

Lunis sighed. "You have no idea. People come to expect it from me."

"I can understand how taxing that could be," Faraday agreed. "Let me put in my password, and we can go."

"Cool," Lunis chirped. "Just don't use the password 'beef stew.' It's not stroganoff."

CHAPTER FORTY-SEVEN

Paris hadn't been on Roya Lane for more than a minute when someone shouted her name. She turned to find her Aunt Sophia striding in her direction. It always filled her with delight to see the dragonrider boldly walking in her armor with her sword at her side. Paris could hardly believe that the majestic leader of the dragonriders was related to her. She wondered if she'd feel the same way when her mother was back in action and striding around as a Warrior for the House of Fourteen and her father was hunting down demons. Something told her that she had many more prideful moments to come.

"Hey, I'm glad I caught you." Sophia approached with a smile. "You weren't answering your phone."

"Yeah, that whole having them being addictive has kept me away from mine," Paris stated. "I can't afford to lose hours scrolling through Instagram."

Sophia nodded. "Yeah, but I wanted to tell you that Papa Creola has invited Clark and me to see Liv and Stefan this morning. Do you want to join?"

Paris let out a squeak of glee. "Of course I do! That's amazing. It seems that they are getting better then?"

"Yes, I think, knowing my sister, that she could have popped back into this world and gone back to work the very hour that she returned. But Papa Creola is cautious. He can't afford to lose her again. I'm sure all sorts of time-related issues have been a problem in her absence, and she'll have to fix them."

"I'm sure." Paris chewed on her lip, suddenly overwhelmed that her mother was Father Time's right-hand woman.

"Hey," Sophia said, consolingly, "None of that is more important than spending time with you. I know Liv can't make up for the years of yours that she lost, but if anyone tries, it will be your mother."

"Oh, I know." The unexpected tenderness of the moment struck Paris. "I'm fine on that…just…"

"Just what?" Sophia gave her a speculative look.

"I'm tired," Paris admitted. "I had a long night and need to go to see Mortimer about this planetary alignment that's happening tonight. I have to help Uncle John figure out what someone's planning in the FLEA jail and hopefully stop it."

"Oh, you will," Sophia stated with confidence. "After this morning's reunion, Lunis, Faraday, and the Rogue Riders are off to stop this signal broadcasting from the satellite. Then we're having a big party to celebrate our victory."

Paris smiled, grateful for the boost of confidence. "Thanks. I'm grateful to have your help with the phone issue. I guess Lunis and Faraday are working on the software. The squirrel said that would take some setup."

Sophia nodded. "Yeah, and I'm sorry for any bad habits that my dragon teaches your companion." The dragonrider put her arm around Paris' shoulder and steered her toward the Official Brownie Headquarters.

"Now, why don't you tell me about this long night you had, and I'll accompany you to see Mortimer. I could use some Brownie time before our reunion with Liv. Seeing those guys always resurrects my hope for humanity. They focus on the best things humans do instead of the very worst, and oddly enough, they're always happy because of it. I think there's a lot to be learned from those little elves."

CHAPTER FORTY-EIGHT

"I see why Sophia doesn't let you have powdered donuts." Faraday's cheeks caught the wind as he talked, making him feel like he swallowed a cloud.

Lunis dove sharply, like a missile, making Faraday think they'd crash into the Pacific Ocean. He gripped the saddle for dear life.

"Oh, wait until I crash from the sugar." Lunis spiraled through the air.

Faraday flattened himself to the dragon, knowing that the centrifugal force would keep him pinned in place but doubting science at that moment. "Can we be on the ground when you have this sugar crash?"

"Come on," Lunis teased, straightening out and coasting over the blue waters along Malibu. "I thought you wanted a flight lesson before we went up to the stratosphere."

"I wanted to survive long enough to get up there, as well." Faraday barely opened his mouth from the rush of air knocking him in the face.

"It was a good idea to get the hang of flying first," Lunis offered.

"It's one of the major components to an astronaut's training," Faraday replied. "Getting used to the gravitational force takes time."

The blue dragon lifted his front right leg up to his face as if checking his imaginary watch. "We have about an hour to do a crash course."

"Can you not call it that?" Faraday remembered why he liked being on the ground rather than climbing trees like most squirrels.

"Crash, you mean?" Lunis teased.

"Yeah, and I need to get back soon to check on the updates running on the computer," Faraday said as Lunis swerved around some kites tourists were flying on the beach. His current glamour prevented mortals from seeing him. Otherwise, the kids would be getting more of a show than watching their nylon dragons soaring in the wind.

"I hope your computer is okay," Lunis said, suddenly serious.

"Yeah, I'm sure it's fine. Why?" Faraday asked.

"I was hoping that it didn't crash!" Lunis laughed loudly, making Faraday bounce in the air from his movement.

"Oh, good one…" Faraday said darkly.

"You know, maybe you can help me install a speaker on my back so I can listen to music when I'm cruising."

Faraday closed his eyes as they got dangerously close to a cliff, soaring around Point Dume. "Yeah, I can do that."

"Awesome!" Lunis cheered. "Then I can listen to my favorite band. The Crash Test Dummies."

"When you find a person's weakness, you exploit it, don't you?" Faraday dared to open his eyes to find they were gaining altitude.

"This is for your good," Lunis stated. "The best way to prepare you for what's coming is through desensitization training."

"If you give me a heart attack, I won't be able to go on the mission." Faraday's little squirrel heart was beating faster than he could ever remember.

"Oh, you can't die," Lunis encouraged, suddenly sounding sensitive. "You have to save the world. You're the only one who can."

"Well, I don't know about all that." Faraday tucked his chin as the dragon turned into a nosedive.

"Repeat after me," Lunis urged. "My name is Faraday So-And-So. Sorry, I didn't catch your last name."

The squirrel laughed. "My name is Faraday So-And-So. Sorry, I didn't catch your last name."

"Nice one," Lunis sang. "My name is Faraday, and I'm going to save the world."

"My name is Faraday, and I'm going to save the world," he repeated.

"I'm going to save the world because I'm good enough, I'm smart enough and doggone it, people like me," Lunis stated.

"Can we stop this?" Faraday asked, feeling his stomach turning upside down from the free fall they were currently doing.

"No," Lunis answered, straightening out before they crashed into a building.

"I'm Faraday, and I'm going to save the world because it's what we do," Lunis continued.

"I'm going to save the world because it's what we do," Faraday stated with growing confidence.

"And the world is always worth saving."

The squirrel repeated the phrase. "And the world is always worth saving."

The dragon swiftly landed on the road outside the electronics repair shop. "Good. Now how do you feel?"

"Better." Faraday's confidence had risen now that he'd taken his first flight on a dragon and survived.

"Good," Lunis chirped. "Now you better save the world because I have Justin Bieber concert tickets and I'm not missing it because the absence of love destroyed this planet."

"I'm not sure that the destruction of love will end the world," Faraday stated. "It will just make for a really sad planet."

"Have you heard Justin's music?" Lunis questioned. "If there is no love, then there is no Bieber. Then there will be one angry dragon, and the world will be in trouble. Fix this problem, squirrel, or I'm going to eat you."

CHAPTER FORTY-NINE

"That's incredible," Sophia said when Paris told her about her blood regrowing the Bewilder Forest. "I can't wait to see it."

"That's right. You can visit Happily Ever After College, right?" Paris asked as they stood in front of the brick wall where the invisible entrance to the Official Brownie Headquarters would soon appear since they'd announced their presence—looking like loons talking to a solid wall.

Sophia nodded. "Yes, I have special macaroons that open a portal to the college for me, although I'm not a fairy or godmother nor work for Happily Ever After."

Paris laughed. "Of course it's special cookies. What's up with those silly fairies and their sweets?"

"I don't know. I'd prefer having some beef jerky that opened the portal, but that's the dragonrider in me."

"And being a magician too," Paris offered. "I think we prefer salty and protein-rich things."

"Like cheese," Sophia said dreamily as the door appeared.

"Yes, exactly like cheese," Paris agreed.

"The college has gone through many evolutions in the last two decades." Sophia knelt to crawl through the small entrance to the

Brownie office. "I think that under the current Saint Valentine it will find its place, but it's been stumbling to get there."

Paris copied her movement, waiting for her turn to crawl through. "I agree, but he has to deal with old traditions and resistance from the board. I think what happens in the next period will be defining."

"There's a power struggle," Sophia mumbled, crawling through the small door. She straightened once through and turned to help Paris inside, although she didn't need it, and almost moved as gracefully as her aunt. "When there's a fight for power, the results create a ripple effect. Whoever wins this battle will champion the war."

"War?" Paris questioned, brushing off her black plants. "There's no war."

Sophia gave her a sympathetic look that seemed to say, "Oh, bless your heart."

"There's always a war," Sophia offered. "It's just that usually it's fought with things more dangerous than guns—magic."

"Bophia Seaufont!" a Brownie exclaimed, running at them, his hands waving in the air and ears flopping.

"Ticker!" Sophia cheered, hugging what was probably the most adorable creature Paris had set eyes upon. "It's good to see you!"

"Tou yoo!" The Brownie released Sophia, looking rather curiously at Paris. "Lot Niv?"

"No, this is her daughter, Paris Beaufont," Sophia explained. "You met her when she was a child and called her Buinevere Geaufont."

Paris was one hundred percent confused and felt like she suddenly didn't understand the English language.

Seeing the confusion on Paris' face, Sophia smiled. "Ticker is Mortimer and his wife, Pricilla's son. He speaks in two-word phrases and reverses the first letters of them. It's a sweet quirk that you'll come to treasure, I'm sure."

The Brownie bowed low to Paris. "Pello Haris!"

She giggled, surprised that the creature somehow got even more adorable. "Hello, Ticker. A pleasure to meet you. I'm here to see your father about something. Is he in his office?"

"Yes, yes!" Ticker answered.

"Great, well, I'll pop back and see him, then," Paris said.

"I'll catch up with Ticker." Sophia sat on the floor and patted the spot next to her for the Brownie to join her.

Paris nodded and headed down the hallway, impressed by the image of the noble and majestic leader of the dragonriders sitting crossed-legged on the floor and chatting with a little house elf. The Beaufonts were really something, and she was grateful to be one of them.

CHAPTER FIFTY

Mortimer was bouncing a ball against the wall next to the door when Paris entered. He caught it and smiled at her.

"Paris Beaufont, fairy godmother in training at Happily Ever After College. It is lovely to see you."

"You too," she replied. "I met your son. He's delightful."

Mortimer blushed, his ears perking up. "Why, thank you. And I can guess the reason that you're here. Tonight is the planetary alignment."

"Yes, thanks for your help. Were you able to find the mirrors placed around the FLEA jail or better yet, who was doing it?" she asked hopefully.

A frown rose on his face. "Unfortunately, none of my Brownies saw who was placing them. The planetary alignment has already started and therefore, it appears to be hiding whoever is putting the mirrors around the Fairy Law Enforcement Agency jail."

Paris gasped. "Oh, I didn't realize that it had already started."

"The planetary alignment is in process for many moons before it achieves the full position," Mortimer explained. "It's during the exact alignment that one can harness the strange magic. Before that and afterward, it simply hides things that normally are visible."

"Like someone sneaking around the FLEA jail and placing mirrors," Paris guessed.

Mortimer nodded. "Yes, and I'm sure due to your uncle, Detective John Nicholson, you'll know that there are wards that prevent invisibility spells in the FLEA jail."

Paris slumped. "But I bet they don't work as well during the planetary alignment."

"Unfortunately, your wager is correct."

"It appears that someone has been working on this for quite some time," Paris muttered.

"Maybe or they are capitalizing on the event. I have some more bad news," Mortimer began with a grave expression on his face. "During the hour of perfect alignment, not only will whatever is desired be hidden from view, but all the wards for the jail will be down."

"All of the wards?" Paris questioned in shock. "Uncle John has to be aware of this."

"Possibly but we both know the truth about your uncle," Mortimer said, a hint in his voice.

Paris lowered his chin. "You're aware that he's not a fairy…"

Mortimer nodded. "I'm also aware that he's putting more security measures in place, but I'm not sure how effective they will be."

"Which is exactly why this person or organization is picking the planetary alignment. They have to be trying to break someone out of jail."

"Yes, that's my conclusion too. Although we were able to find many a mirror and take them down, as I warned before, finding them is difficult. I'm not confident that we got rid of all of them."

"Which means?" Paris asked.

"Which means that whatever they're trying to hide probably will be," Mortimer explained, disappointment in his tone.

"Right…"

"But!" Mortimer squealed, a bit of hope in his voice making her perk up. "Because we found some of the mirrors, there's a chance that whatever they want to hide can be seen during certain times."

"Like, maybe if whatever it is moves out of the path of the mirror's refractions of light or something?" Paris guessed, not at all certain that she understood all this mirror business.

"That's my thought," Mortimer answered. "Or maybe there's a light or a spell or a tool you can use to make what's hidden visible. Not having all the mirrors in place puts a hole in the magic meant to hide whatever it was, but I'm not sure how to see through those holes. I apologize for the bad pun."

Paris found herself laughing. "That's okay. Bad puns are always welcome."

"I'm also sorry that we couldn't be of more help," Mortimer stated, bouncing the ball in his hands. "We really do like to be able to help the Beaufonts."

"And you have," Paris said gratefully. "I know more than I did before and hopefully it's enough to help Uncle John to stop whatever is happening. He's done so much for me. It will be nice if I can help him with his job for once instead of causing trouble for him."

Paris hadn't really thought about that sentiment until that moment. Before, she'd been motivated to find out what was happening at the FLEA jail, encouraged by her demon blood that despised wrongdoing.

However, in the past, although she'd meant to help by going after criminals, she'd usually only caused more problems for Uncle John. She hoped that this time she made his job easier and stopped the criminal activity about to go down at the jail.

And as a bonus, she'd find out what was afoot, satisfying her curiosity. She had no clue who was trying to escape, but she wasn't going to let anything stop her from finding out.

First, though, she needed a way to see them… That was the tricky part since they were at the eleventh hour with the planetary alignment almost upon them.

CHAPTER FIFTY-ONE

"Oh, good, I needed to see you," Subner said when Paris and Sophia entered the Fantastical Armory.

"Me?" Paris pointed at her chest in surprise. "Did you have an insult you were looking forward to giving me?"

The angry elf shook his head of greasy black hair. "Not you. Her." He pointed at Sophia beside her.

"Oh, that makes more sense," Paris muttered.

"I have a mission for you after you help the squirrel stop the signal broadcasting from the satellite," Subner said to Sophia.

"Wow, you all know everything all the time, don't you?" Paris asked, impressed.

"I know that you could irritate a monk full of patience to jump off a cliff," Subner grumbled.

"I probably could," Paris stated proudly. "What's your superpower?"

"Ignoring dimwits." He waved Sophia over. "Let me give you the details. Then you can go and have your reunion, although I can't understand why anyone cares that the magicians are back. Fifteen years of peace and now it's over."

Sophia shook her head, obviously used to Subner's bad attitude.

"In the meantime, you can come over and chat with us," a familiar voice sang at Paris' back. It was a voice she didn't know well but felt etched on her soul.

She turned to find Mama Jamba and Papa Creola lounging in a new sitting area in the far corner of the Fantastical Armory. The cozy space looked out of sorts in the store with its weapons lining the wall and glass cases with strange artifacts.

Mother Nature and Papa Creola were seated in floral patterned armchairs. Between them was a round coffee table with a tray of tea and cookies. Mama Jamba was wearing a white tracksuit and a sneaky grin. Her bouffant bluish-gray hair was perfectly in place and probably had an entire can of hair spray on it. She set her teacup with blackbirds on it on the saucer and smiled sweetly at Paris.

"Oh, where are my manners?" Mama Jamba asked. "You need a seat if you're joining us." She spun her finger, and another floral patterned armchair appeared.

"Thanks." Paris took the seat Mother Nature had conjured for her.

"Don't get too comfortable." Papa Creola eyed his tea with disdain. "Clark will be here in six minutes."

"The perfect amount of time for us to chat," Mama Jamba sang.

Paris didn't know what they were supposed to talk about. Maybe she should casually mention the weather or complain about the lack of rain or how the year felt like it was passing so quickly. She laughed to herself, thinking this was probably not the best audience for such a conversation.

"Would you like a cup of tea?" Mama Jamba pointed at the tray. "Maybe a cookie?"

"No, thank you." Paris suddenly felt nervous in the presence of the two gods.

"Nice work with the Bewilder Forest," Mama Jamba said. "I look forward to seeing what it becomes. I love a new forest."

"You have more forests than a socialite has pairs of shoes," Papa Creola grumbled and set down his cup of tea. He was wearing a t-shirt that said, "The time you enjoy wasting isn't wasted time."

"That's a funny shirt for you to be wearing," Paris pointed out, indicating his tie-dyed shirt.

He glanced down and grimaced. "I don't have any choice in the matter. My current form is only comfortable in organic bamboo t-shirts with hippie phrases. It makes me even more sour than usual."

"Oh, I think rainbow colors suit you, Papa." Mama Jamba smiled, holding out her hand and looking directly at Paris. "Now, I have something for you."

"For me?" Paris was surprised.

Mama Jamba's eyes darted to the side as she pursed her lips. "Where did I put that..."

"Maybe it's in one of your precious forests," Papa Creola muttered, looking especially grumpy.

"Are you okay?" Paris felt silly asking the father of time if he was all right.

"He's fine." Mama Jamba waved her off. "Papa is sad that Liv will be leaving here soon. He's worried about her, but I assessed her myself, and she's getting ready."

"My mother will be able to leave here soon?" Paris was again surprised, and this time elated. She couldn't wait for her parents to reenter the real world. For everyone to know that they were back. For them to walk down Roya Lane with her in the sunshine...for their lives to officially start.

"Apparently." Papa Creola crossed his arms over his chest, not at all looking happy about the prospect that excited Paris more than anything. "I don't think she's ready."

"I contend that she is," Mama Jamba argued. "They both are. Your concern about their mental health after the ordeal and time jumps is understandable, but at this point, it's only you being an overly protective papa bear."

"Don't use that phrase," he scolded.

"Overly protective?" Mama Jamba said innocently, her hand still outstretched although her attention was on the old hippie elf.

"Papa Bear," he corrected.

"Well, you love her more than any of my children," Mama Jamba countered.

"She makes my job easier is all," Papa Creola stated.

"Then one might say you'd want her back in action as soon as possible," Mama Jamba said sneakily.

"I do," Papa Creola replied. "I don't want my best to have her head fried because she's jumped fifteen years into the future. She'll be useless to me if she doesn't assimilate properly and her brain turns to Jell-O."

"We both know that Liv Beaufont will be fine." Mama Jamba reached out and patted Papa Creola's knee. "She was fine when born. Stronger after her parents' death. And completely unstoppable since she took the role as Warrior for the House of Fourteen." She looked at Paris and shook her head. "It's tough on us when our children are ready to fly from the nest, even if they've done it several times before. Your mother fell from the nest and disappeared into another world, as you know. Papa is afraid of losing her again, and that's understandable."

"I'm not," he grumbled, picking up a cookie and taking a bite as if it had done something rude to him.

"We appreciate those we love more when we've lost them, sometimes." Mama Jamba's attention was still on Paris.

"You said you had something for her." Papa Creola pointed at Paris with the cookie in his hand. "Why don't you stop leaving the halfling in suspense. Clark will be here in two minutes."

"Oh, that's right." Mama Jamba held out her hand, her other one tapping her chin. "Now, I need to remember where I put that lovely object. I last saw it a couple of centuries ago."

"The left drawer on the right, under the silk gloves." Papa Creola stuck the rest of the cookie in his mouth.

Mama Jamba brightened. "Why, thank you, Papa. Who says you're not helpful?"

"I've lost track," Papa Creola replied. "Bunch of ingrates, they all are."

"Here it is." A small, flat silver disc appeared In Mama Jamba's hand, like a compact mirror. It had etching on its front. "I think you'll need this." She extended her hand for Paris to take the shiny object.

On the front were the words, "She believed she could, so she did."

"This is for me?" Paris found a seam in the middle of the sleek object. "What is it?"

"A mirror, of course," Mama Jamba stated with a proud smile.

Paris opened it to find that both sides of the object had a reflective surface. She spied her confused expression in the mirror. Looking at Mama Jamba, she tilted her head. "Why are you giving this to me?"

"Oh, I was under the impression that you'd need a way to see hidden things." Mama Jamba picked up her teacup. "What better way to see that which the mirrors are hiding than with a mirror."

"The planetary alignment," Paris said with a gasp. "This will help me see?"

Mama Jamba nodded, sat back in her seat, and sipped.

Paris looked back at the mirror, wishing the one-and-a-half-inch surface was a little wider. It was about like looking through binoculars. She wouldn't be able to see a lot at once, but thankfully it gave her a way to see in the FLEA jail.

Shutting the compact, Paris smiled. "Thanks. This helps. I don't suppose you can tell me what's going on in the jail or what we're facing."

"I can't," Mama Jamba stated.

"She won't," Papa Creola corrected and took another cookie. "Clark is here, which means it's time for the reunion."

Paris turned to see her uncle entering the Fantastical Armory. His expression was suspense mixed with anticipation as he glanced between Sophia on the far side of the shop and Paris. It had been a long fifteen years for the siblings, and Paris knew they had both been looking forward to this moment.

CHAPTER FIFTY-TWO

Paris couldn't imagine the emotions building in Sophia and Clark as they descended the hundreds of stairs to the bottom basement of the Fantastical Armory. For her parents, it had only been several long confusing days since they saw the dragonrider and the Councilor for the House of Fourteen.

For Sophia and Clark, it had been fifteen years.

Fifteen years where they didn't know where Liv and Stefan were or if they'd ever be able to return. Fifteen years where they were separated from Paris and Uncle John and everyone else, needing to protect the halfling from the Deathly Shadow. Fifteen years where they couldn't see their best friend—Liv Beaufont seemed to be everyone's best friend and Paris knew why. She loved people for who they were and brought out the best in them.

Sophia and Clark walked at a steady pace in front of Paris. She read their body language and could sense they were trying not to run down the flights of stairs separating them from their sister.

Having learned their history, Paris knew that after her grandparents' death, Liv had left her family—unable to accept that it was an accident. That's when she'd met Plato and Uncle John. She'd been away from her family for five years before Clark asked her to return to the House of Fourteen. That reunion had been emotional, but it had nothing on this one. Paris prepared herself, knowing that there wouldn't be a lack of tears.

Sophia, who had been holding back, ran once the light of the basement hit her face. As before, Papa Creola had glamoured it to look like the apartment above John's Electronics Repair shop. It was white and bright and open and light, making it easy to see as Liv ran into her sister's arms, hugging her with a force that spoke of her love.

Sophia's blonde hair waved in the air as she ran, closing her arms around her sister. She pressed Liv in so tightly that the Warrior squealed. Then there were tears—as Paris knew there would be. So many tears.

Clark was pushing away droplets from his face as he threw his arms around the pair, hugging them both. Paris' father looked on the verge of letting a tear spill as he watched the reunion from the sidelines. He gave Paris a caring look as she took the last step, also watching from a distance.

Sophia wiggled out of Clark's and Liv's arms, her hands on her sister's face, looking at her with astonishment. "I-I-I can't believe you're back...and you haven't changed a single bit."

"I was only gone a day," Liv said through a constricted throat.

"Not in our world," Clark replied.

Liv nodded, her face still in Sophia's hands as if the dragonrider was afraid to let her go—as though she'd disappear again. "I know... I'm sorry..."

"There's no reason to apologize." Clark stared at her in awe. "We're happy that you're back. Liv, this world isn't the same when you're not in it."

If Liv was holding back before, she let go then, tears spilling from her eyes in a rush. "I can't imagine what you've all been through the last fifteen years. Changing everything for us. Protecting Paris. Doing everything to get us back."

"There was never a moment when it wasn't worth it," Clark said. He had to deal with the most change, marrying someone to protect Liv's position in the House of Fourteen.

"We wanted you back." Sophia pulled her hands away from Liv's face to wipe her own tears. She glanced up, looking at Stefan for the first time. "And you too."

Stefan grinned and strode forward to hug the dragonrider. "I know that I'll always pale in comparison to Liv. How could I not? But it's good to be missed."

When they'd separated, Paris was surprised to see her father hug Clark as well, patting him affectionately on the back.

"This world in the way of demons isn't the same without you, man," Clark said when they'd pulled apart. "No one can control that population like you."

Stefan laughed, breaking the tension. "Well, it takes one to know one."

Now that the news had spilled that Paris Beaufont had demon blood, it had also gotten out that she'd gotten it from her father—a fact that he'd covered up. However, there was nothing for anyone to worry about since he'd obtained a cure, and she had in her unique way too.

"Are you pretending not to be here?" Liv asked Paris, gracefully arriving at her side and pulling her in for a hug.

"Just giving you all the opportunity for the reunion you deserve," Paris replied when her mother released her into her father's arms.

He hugged her tightly, and she didn't think she'd ever tire of having her parents' affection.

"I can't believe it's been fifteen years." Liv looked her siblings over. "You two look the same, unlike this one." She indicated Paris, her father's arm still around her shoulders.

"Well, we were full-grown already," Sophia teased. "And I have the chi of the dragon to thank for my youthful appearance."

"And Clark has his regimen and a bazillion vitamins and sunscreen to thank," Liv joked.

Everyone laughed, including Clark, who was looking around the place.

"This looks like home," he said affectionately.

"Yes, but it doesn't feel like it," Liv replied. "I can't wait to return."

"It sounds like that will be soon," Paris offered. "Papa Creola mentioned it."

"Yeah, but he's not happy about it," Liv stated. "Subner will be ecstatic to have me gone though. I look for at least a dozen ways to get under his skin every single day hoping that he'll pack my bags for me when it's time to leave."

"You don't have anything to pack," Clark said seriously as if Liv wasn't joking.

Liv grinned, also putting her arm around Paris' shoulders on her other side. "No, I have everything I need right here."

"Now that you two are back, we have everything we need." Sophia fondly looked at her family. "We're all back together."

"Hopefully we always will be." Clark wrapped his arm around Sophia's shoulder and regarded Liv, Stefan, and Paris thoughtfully.

"We will," Liv said. "Forever and always."

"Familia est sempiternum." Paris automatically said the phrase written on the far wall that was the Beaufont family motto.

Liv smiled at her daughter. "Familia est sempiternum."

CHAPTER FIFTY-THREE

The plains of Oklahoma were a strange sight lined with dragons suited up for battle. Beside each unique dragon of varying colors were their riders, fierce expressions on their faces.

Faraday sat in a specially made harness on Lunis' back, his computer secured in front of him. There wouldn't normally be enough space for the squirrel and the rider on the dragon's back. However, Lunis had a great ability to supersize himself by harnessing the power of the moon. That was one reason they were taking off to stop the signal broadcasting from the satellite at night.

Not only was the hour approaching for the perfect planetary alignment, but it was also the night of a full moon. The timing couldn't be better, and in some ways, it was very problematic. For whoever was planning something at the FLEA jail, the timing was perfect. For Paris, it posed many problems.

Faraday hoped that she'd be successful in stopping whatever was going to happen. If anyone could, it would be her. His mission was to stop the signal broadcasting to cell phones. Then people worldwide would be released from their cellular addiction, and hopefully love would have a chance to flourish once more.

Easily the size of a Boeing 747, Lunis stood in front of the other dragons and riders, eclipsing them with his massive frame. Sophia had handpicked the riders that would be accompanying them based on their skills. They were a mix of members from the Dragon Elite and Rogue Riders since protecting Lunis, Sophia, and Faraday from the drones was supremely important. If anything happened to them, they'd lose their opportunity to take down the signal. Faraday felt the pressure on his shoulders, but he wanted this victory. He needed it.

Wilder and his dragon, Simi could harness the wind. Alina and her dragon, Frost possessed powerful ice magic. Evan and Coral were good with water, but more importantly, they had superior combat skills. Last there was Mark and his dragon Lightning, who could shoot electricity. There were also half a dozen other dragons and riders who would serve as a shield while the others took an offensive stance against the drones.

Under the starry sky, Sophia strode in front of the line of dragons. "There are roughly six drones stationed between where we need to be and the satellite. It's believed that as soon as Faraday starts to intercept the signal from the satellite that the drones will go into attack mode. It's unclear how long it will take for Faraday to do what he needs to stop the signal. That's why you all have such a crucial role."

Sophia paused, looking up at the three dragons and riders that would be attacking the drones. "Wilder, Alina, and Mark will take off first and hopefully be able to take out the drones before they become a problem."

She continued forward, glancing at the other dragons and their riders. "You all will be the second to launch and provide a barrier between us and the drones. Remember that we're flying high and fast. We won't be able to get into the mesosphere where the drones are. That's why formation and range are important. Lunis is a big target, and therefore you all shielding us is critical. Stay on the comms and relay all important information to each other. We are only as good as our communications. Are there any questions?"

"Yeah, I got one." Lunis looked down at his rider with a murderous expression. "Did you call me fat?"

CHAPTER FIFTY-FOUR

"No one is getting out of here unless they go through me." Uncle John stood like a wall at the front of the Fairy Law Enforcement Agency jail.

"Are you sure about this?" Paris held the mirror that Mama Jamba had given her in her hands, rotating it to scan the front hallway.

"We've been over this, Pare. I know you worry about me, but I'm military trained and have been in war." He held up his fists. "These are lethal weapons."

Paris laughed. Her uncle was strong, but he was also a mortal, didn't have any magic, and they were dealing with a very magical situation with the prime time of the planetary alignment almost upon them. They'd decided to keep the number of guards at the jail to a minimum.

Someone had been getting into the jail and placing the mirrors, which made Uncle John think they had a double agent helping from the inside. Since having a guard who was potentially working for the enemy could pose a huge risk, Uncle John had decided it was best to give the whole staff the night off. Only those he trusted would be in the jail that night patrolling. Unfortunately, there were few on that list.

Uncle John turned to King Rudolf and Lee, the assassin baker. "You two know what you're doing tonight?"

"Shaming the prisoners, telling them what a drain they are on society." Lee slapped a baton into her outstretched hand.

"Finding out where the fairy in Cell Block B hid the treasure they stole from my vault," Rudolf answered.

Uncle John shook his head. "It would be best if you didn't talk to any of the prisoners. King Rudolf, I want you patrolling the eastern corridors."

The fae held up both his hands. "Is east right or left?"

"It's east." Lee pointed down the hallway closest to Rudolf. "It's that way."

King Rudolf peered down the dark corridor, the walls and floors all black. "It looks scary down there."

"It's a jail," Lee said. "Full of criminals. It's not Disney World."

Rudolf shivered. "Disney World is scarier than a jail. People are wearing transitional lenses there. Like, how did those people not get the memo that those were never a good fashion choice?"

"I think they were going for practicality," Paris offered.

The king shook his head. "One must never choose practicality over fashion. Never. It's like dresses with pockets. Why don't you put on a trash bag already? Promise me you'll never wear a dress with pockets, Paris."

"I want to promise you that I'll never wear a dress," Paris muttered, thinking of the one she had to have made for her graduation at Happily Ever After College.

Uncle John glanced at his watch. "Although I appreciate the opportunity for humor during this stressful time, we are approaching the planetary alignment." He pointed at the other corridor. "Lee, I'd like you patrolling the western side. Both of you keep an eye out for anything suspicious. Keep a count on the prisoners, ensuring that they're all in their cells.

"The extra security wards will be down for a full hour. Each cell is manually locked, and none of the prisoners can use magic inside of their cells. However, the hallways along them are open areas. If someone is trying to sneak someone out, they'll be able to use magic to unlock the cells."

"And for the hour of perfect planetary alignment," Paris added, "Whoever or whatever is trying to hide will be entirely invisible." She held up the mirror. "This is the only way to see anything."

Uncle John nodded with a look of remorse. "Since Mother Nature gave it to Paris, she's going to be patrolling with that. Although I'd prefer for my niece not to be here tonight, she won't listen to reason."

"I faced the Deathly Shadow," she argued. "I think I've earned the right to be here. And you need those who you can trust here tonight, and as we've learned, that list is short."

He sighed. "It's true. Only you three are in the jail tonight, along with the prisoners and me. If you see anyone else, they aren't authorized to be here and are automatically the culprit we're looking for."

"Okay, so we're looking for someone invisible doing something that we don't know," King Rudolf stated matter-of-factly. "Great. Seems like a regular Tuesday afternoon at the Sweetwater mansion."

Uncle John sighed again. The vein on his forehead that surfaced when he was stressed appeared. "Unfortunately, being vigilant is all we can do. We know someone is planning something. They have to be. The time to do it is in the next hour. It's a jail, so it has to be a break. All we have to do is keep the prisoners in their cells and hopefully find the person behind this. Then I'll have a cell with their name on it."

CHAPTER FIFTY-FIVE

Agent Ruby wanted to laugh at the absurdity of a fae, a baker, a halfling, and the detective trying to stop him. He overhead their plan from the eastern corridor, already invisible and having snuck into the jail before they cleared it out.

The beginning of the planetary alignment had made it so that Agent Ruby could have moments of invisibility but not for long, and it was extremely draining on magic. That's how he'd been able to sneak into the jail over the last week and place the mirrors. Those objects made it so that for the hour of total planetary alignment, Agent Ruby was completely invisible and without draining any of his magic. That was important because he needed all of his reserves for what he had planned.

Murdering Agent Topaz would take proper setup, and that would take time. Therefore, Agent Ruby had to ensure that the laughable patrols of the jail didn't get in his way. For that, he'd have to plant a diversion.

Detective Nicholson believed that someone was trying to break a prisoner out of there. He'd feed into that belief, and while the clowns were chasing down an inmate on the western side of the jail, Agent Ruby would be taking out Agent Topaz on the eastern corridor. Dead men couldn't talk, which was important since Agent Topaz was the only one who could blow his cover.

Pulling his silver ballpoint pen with the heart-shaped ruby at its end from his pocket, Agent Ruby started down the hallway, considering which criminal let loose would cause the biggest commotion.

CHAPTER FIFTY-SIX

Faraday was grateful that he'd had the flight lesson with Lunis. Getting used to flying on a dragon had taken some practice. He'd adapted to the motion and altitude change meaning that he could concentrate on the task at hand.

Still, the beating of the dragon's wings as they flew higher made Faraday a little sick. He told himself not to look down, knowing they were flying higher than when they'd practiced.

Maybe sensing his unease beside her, Sophia offered him a sympathetic smile. "Leave the flying to us. You focus on taking down that signal once we're in place."

The squirrel gulped, nodding. The air was getting thinner as they climbed higher. Ahead of them was the defensive line of half a dozen dragons and riders. In front of *them* was the offensive line, who were hopefully making quick work of the drones.

In a perfect world, the dragonriders would take out the drones and Faraday would have no trouble disabling the signal. Then they could cruise back down to the ground where the squirrel would be eternally grateful to be on soil, never wanting to leave it again.

"We have a problem," Wilder said over the comms.

Faraday stiffened.

"What's up?" Sophia's voice was in the squirrel's head and right beside him.

"These ain't no normal drones," the dragonrider named Evan said.

"Well, they are protecting a satellite that someone knew we'd have to get close to in order to stop the signal," Sophia reminded them.

"Yeah, we knew they'd try and attack us," Wilder explained.

"But…" Sophia waited for them to fill in the blanks.

"There's a defensive shield around them," Mark stated. "No matter what we do, we can't get past them. Electricity isn't working."

Sophia sighed. "So taking them out is going to be difficult, then."

"It's going to take time to get past the shields," Alina replied.

"We don't have time." Sophia groaned. "We're almost into place."

"Oh, and one other thing," Evan sang casually into the comms.

"What?" Sophia didn't sound as though she was going to like his answer.

"They shoot freaking laser beams," Evan answered. "Hot-ass lasers that can fry an egg in space."

Sophia's and Faraday's eyes connected, fear gripping the squirrel. She gave him a pure look of conviction, and unshakable tenacity radiated from her.

"Don't worry," she encouraged. "Remember, this is what we're here for. Get ready to take out that signal but brace yourself. This is going to be a bumpy ride."

CHAPTER FIFTY-SEVEN

S*omething wasn't right.* Paris took off down the western hallway. She knew they were patrolling the FLEA jail because someone was up to something, so obviously something wasn't right. But she felt like she was missing something—besides the fact that for the next hour, something or someone could be hiding inside the jail.

The plan that she and Uncle John had formulated seemed smart. Since the magical security wards were down, they had manual locks in place. He was guarding the only entrance to the jail. They had two patrols they could trust. Still, Paris couldn't shake the feeling that they weren't thinking of something and it was going to slip by them.

The FLEA jail was a big square with the prisoners' cells in the center and the corridor running along the edge. Earlier, she'd timed a lap, and from the front around the loop, it took Paris three full minutes to get back to the start if she was moving fast. There were one hundred cells, and they were at sixty percent capacity.

Sixty prisoners. Four guards. One hour.

Paris wanted to believe that no one would escape in that hour. But again, she had this nagging feeling that they'd missed something. Walking at an even pace, she held up the compact mirror, rotating to see the area all around her. Nothing showed up in the mirror that wasn't there. It was just walls, bars, and prisoners.

She sighed, wondering if maybe they were wrong and nothing would happen during the planetary alignment. Possibly whoever was behind it was deterred when they put their plan into effect to protect the jail. Perhaps they didn't want to get caught and would give up.

"We got a runner!" Lee yelled from around the corner.

King Rudolf darted past her, sprinting from the eastern corridor. "I'm coming to the rescue."

Paris took off in that direction, her pulse suddenly racing.

CHAPTER FIFTY-EIGHT

It was like taking candy from a baby, Agent Ruby thought with evil delight as he heard the three incompetent and poor excuses for guards run toward the western corridor. Using magic, he opened the cell of one of the most dangerous criminals in the FLEA jail, freeing them. Then, as invisible as the wind, he strode right past the patrols as they ran for the commotion.

Getting Screaming Sasha back in her cell wouldn't be easy. The villain couldn't use her ability inside the magic-proof cage. None of the prisoners could. Now that she was out of her cell and roaming free in the corridor, her screams were like assaults from iron-clad fists.

Thankfully, Agent Ruby would be well out of earshot and not affected. That was one reason he'd picked Screaming Sasha to let free for this diversion. Her cell was on the opposite side of Agent Topaz's. Furthermore, the angry fairy's screams would cover up Agent Topaz's when he fought to take his last breath.

It was all going to plan.

With a wicked grin, Agent Ruby casually strode for the eastern corridor. He had fifty-five minutes remaining before the planetary alignment was over, his invisibility went away, and the magical security wards were back in the jail. It was plenty of time to do what he'd come there for—as long as nothing went awry.

CHAPTER FIFTY-NINE

"How much do you know about Einstein?" Lunis asked Faraday casually as if they were hanging out at a café and not gaining altitude and encountering deadly drones.

"I've studied his theories extensively," Faraday muttered, trying to concentrate on homing in on the satellite's signal. "Why?'

"Well, because we're venturing out into space so it has me contemplating such things," Lunis replied.

"This is a setup," Sophia commented, looking sideways at the squirrel. "Get ready for it."

"I mean, I don't know much about Einstein," Lunis continued. "Except that he developed a theory about space, well, and about time too!"

Faraday was surprised at the laugh that popped out his mouth. He couldn't believe that as they were swerving through clouds and approaching laser-firing drones that the giant dragon was spouting off jokes. It made him feel suddenly more at ease, and he found his claws typing faster—his focus more attuned to his task at hand...or rather at paw.

"That one was especially bad." Sophia hunkered lower on her dragon. "We're almost in position, team. How are the drones?"

"About like Lunis' jokes," Evan replied over the comms. "Especially bad."

"Their aim is impressively good," Wilder added.

"And by impressively, that means I got a haircut that I wasn't planning on," Mark stated.

"Have you been able to penetrate their shield yet?" Sophia asked as they broke through a thick blanket of clouds and the rays of the moon shone on them. The layers of dragons and riders became visible in the distance as well as the drones. If Faraday had Paris' or Sophia's vision, he could probably see the satellite, but he didn't need that to track its signal.

"If I can get closer, I think I can disable them," Alina answered.

"Then we can fry those babies," Mark added.

"If that doesn't work, I'm sending a tornado at them and knocking them out of the sky," Wilder declared.

Sophia chewed on her lip. "I think there are potential hazards to that scenario."

"Which is why we'll try avoiding it," Wilder replied. "Wind is a fickle thing and hard to control, but I can at least use some gusts to throw off their aim. It's saved Evan's butt a few times already."

Evan laughed over the comms. "Hey, laser tag is only fun if you narrowly miss getting hit."

"Okay, well, you all stay safe and try to knock those things out before they do any damage," Sophia ordered. "We're in place. Defensive line, use your shields to protect us because for the next part, we're sitting ducks."

The six Rogue Riders moved into position above them, forming a wall between Lunis, Faraday, Sophia, and the drones. Flying around them were the offensive line, darting away from red lasers. It wouldn't take long before the drones figured out they had multiple targets. Then it probably wouldn't be a moment longer before they figured out that the huge dragon was the one intercepting the signal they were supposed to protect.

Sophia looked down at Faraday as they hovered in place in the thin, cold air. Thankfully a spell protected them from the frigid temperatures and lack of oxygen. The spell couldn't last long, like their safety from the lasers. It was a race to get the signal down before the many dangers took them down.

"All right, it's all on you now." Sophia had a look of pure confidence in her eyes. "Do what you came here for."

CHAPTER SIXTY

The scream that filled the air was unlike anything Paris had heard before. It made her head feel like it might explode. Her teeth ached in her jaw. Her blood vibrated.

Paris ran after King Rudolf, streaking by Uncle John stationed by the entrance.

"Someone let Screaming Sasha out," he said, his eyes full of urgency.

"Stay in your position," Paris urged. "I'll find them."

"Get her back in her cell!" Uncle John yelled to King Rudolf.

"I'm on it!" he called, rounding the corner to the western corridor.

Paris held out the mirror as she ran, looking for anything in it that she didn't see with her two eyes. If a prisoner was out, as they'd assumed would happen, then someone let them loose, and the only way anyone was leaving was through Uncle John. Hopefully, she would find them first.

Rounding the corner, she saw the source of the scream. It was a large fairy woman who Paris could tell was rather obese, even in the unflattering jumpsuit uniform. Her long hot pink hair was sitting in a high ponytail on the top of her head. What grabbed Paris' attention was the actual visual of the woman's scream.

When she opened her mouth, red beads of light shot from it like gravel swept up in the wind and blasted Lee straight in the chest. Not only was the scream so loud and piercing that it hurt Paris' ears from that distance, but it could assault someone—adding injury to insult.

Lee flew back from the attack and landed on her backside, but impressively, the assassin baker wasn't out for more than a moment before she sprang to her feet. The look on her face was full of conviction. "You think a scream is going to take me down? My wife conditioned me to tune out loudmouths."

Rudolf halted a few yards from the fairy who stood squarely in the corridor, her back toward him. Thankfully they had the screaming fairy surrounded. Unfortunately, she looked like a force to be reckoned with.

CHAPTER SIXTY-ONE

Halting in front of Agent Topaz's jail cell, Agent Ruby started the complex spell that would end the man before him. He wasn't a bad fairy. Actually, he was against the current Saint Valentine and had publicly spoken out to the board about abandoning traditional methods at FGA. Unfortunately for him, that's what made Agent Topaz the perfect scapegoat.

Saint Valentine was suspicious and believed that he had strong dissention within his ranks of agents. Taking him out at Happily Ever After College had failed. Paris Beaufont was supposed to take the fall for murder, which went completely wrong since she'd been proven innocent. When things started to unravel, Agent Topaz was the backup to take the fall for Agent Ruby.

He couldn't afford anything getting in the way of his rise to the FGA's top position. It was all Agent Ruby ever wanted—to be the reigning Saint Valentine. It was his time to rule, and nothing was getting in the way.

Once Agent Topaz was dead, there would be no evidence that connected Agent Ruby to the murder. The love meter had never been lower with the signal broadcasting from the satellite creating phone addictions. Soon the board would overthrow the current Saint Valentine, and Agent Ruby would be the natural replacement.

Finally, Agent Ruby would be able to return FGA and the fairy godmother college to the way it was when they ruled things correctly. Tradition and etiquette would be the pillar of the fairy godmothers' training. Royal matches would be their focus once more. The trashy modern world would become refined and classy again. Agent Ruby's rule as Saint Valentine would restore all that they'd lost.

All he had to do was kill the man before him to guarantee his future. Holding his silver ballpoint pen with the red ruby in the air, Agent Ruby began whispering the complex spell that would make Agent Topaz's death look like a suicide.

The man behind bars didn't know that anyone was standing on the other side of his cell. He'd looked calm sitting on his bed but flinched at the sight of his bedsheets snaking up into the air as if connected to an invisible pulley.

Agent Topaz jumped to his feet, but that would only make hanging him that much easier. He opened his mouth to scream, but Agent Ruby had already put a silencing spell on him. Without magic and his magical instrument—the pocket watch—the man was helpless. Still, he tried to fight as the sheet tied around his neck, but his efforts were futile against Agent Ruby's superior strength and power. He might resist this spell, but in the end, it would be the death of Agent Topaz.

CHAPTER SIXTY-TWO

"Man, those drones are fast!" Evan yelled as he veered to the side on his purple dragon, Coral, to avoid a red laser beam that sliced through the air. It streaked by him, and unfortunately, one of the Rogue Riders behind him had to intercept it with their shield.

Thankfully they were able to dodge to the side on their dragon and take the brunt of the laser before it passed—where it would no doubt hit Lunis.

"How are we doing with getting through the drone's protective shield?" Wilder asked, streaking by on his white dragon, moving fast to avoid attacks.

"I'm working on it," Alina said over the comms. "I think I've figured out a spell that can take them down, but I need another minute."

"You have sixty seconds," Evan called, snaking through the various laser beams shooting through the air. "We're sitting targets unable to pull off any attacks. That's not my style."

"Okay, I think if you try an anti-allowance spell, it should take down the shields," Alina said, breathless, trying to fly and also work combat magic.

"Brilliant solution," Wilder cheered. "Evan, you and I will do the spells. Then Alina and Mark, get ready to blast those drones with ice and electricity."

"Copy that. I'll fry the ones on my side," Mark replied, flying to the east.

"Red Dog, you the man," Evan said, using his nickname for Mark.

"I've stored up a mega blast of ice magic," Alina stated. "I'm ready to freeze these suckers."

Evan worked the anti-allowance spell, finding it much more difficult than he would have thought. Whoever created this magitech knew what they were doing. He was slightly impressed and thoroughly annoyed.

"Shields on my drones are down," Wilder called, diving quickly to avoid being chased.

"Show off," Evan muttered, still working on his drones.

"Problem is," Wilder began. "When you pull down their shields, they get rather angry and chase-y." He was darting around the clouds, two drones hot on his dragon, Simi's, literal tail.

"Yeah, and hitting them just got a lot harder," Mark stated, racing after the drones following Wilder. "Can you get them to hold still? I don't want to hit you with electricity by accident."

"I don't think so," Wilder joked, weaving back and forth on his dragon. "Our communication sort of went to hell when I broke their shield. I think we'll need counseling."

"Well, how about I be your therapist?" Mark let out a victorious laugh as he sent a bolt of electricity to the closest drone, exploding it to bits that unfortunately rained down on the line of Rogue Riders below and Lunis and the others under them.

"Nice one, Red Dog!" Evan cheered as he took the shields down on the remaining drones. "It's showtime, Alina. Freeze those bad boys."

CHAPTER SIXTY-THREE

"Hey, chunkster! You're never going to land a guy if you sound bad as well as look it!" King Rudolf held up his hand as Screaming Sasha spun to face him.

He shot out a sharp stream of ice—the element that the fae controlled best. However, the scream that soared out of Screaming Sasha's mouth met the blast of ice mid-air and knocked it to the concrete floor in broken cubes. She sucked in a breath, and Paris knew another assaulting scream was about to follow.

However, Paris also knew that her job couldn't be to fight the strange fairy. That was what Lee and Rudolf were for. Holding the mirror at arm's length, Paris rotated, quickly trying to assess the area for anything hidden.

Before Screaming Sasha could loose another attack, Lee clobbered her from behind, tackling her to the floor. The prisoner was quite large, but thankfully she wasn't much of a match for Lee. The two rolled, with Screaming Sasha trying to claw Lee's face. However, the assassin baker delivered a few punches to the fairy's face.

"Oh, good one!" Rudolf exclaimed. "Get her in the mouth-hole!"

"Why...don't...you...give...me...a...hand," Lee said between breaths, as Screaming Sasha rolled on top of her, jumping up and down and knocking the air from her chest.

The king of the fae clapped loudly. "You're doing a great job, Lee!"

"I'm going to murder you after I kill this one," Lee threatened as the pink-haired inmate sucked in a breath, her distance from Lee deadly close. If she let out a yell at that range, it would no doubt be a murderous blow.

Thankfully King Rudolf jumped into action. Literally. He leapt forward, kicked Screaming Sasha in the back, and knocked her off Lee.

Paris was worried for her friends. She wanted to help. One look at Uncle John, stationed by the entrance, and she knew what she had to do. He angled to the eastern hallway. "Check it out. I think I heard something."

She nodded, turned her back on the fight, and headed down the dark corridor with the magic mirror her only way of finding who was behind all this.

CHAPTER SIXTY-FOUR

Agent Ruby was running out of time—and energy. Sweat poured down his forehead, and his hand holding the silver ballpoint pen was shaking. The spell had taken longer than he anticipated and depleted his magic fast, making him weak.

He couldn't break his concentration to check the time, but he feared that half the hour had spun by. However, the good news was that Agent Topaz was almost dead.

Due to the silencing spell, he couldn't cry out to alert the patrols of what was happening. However, there was no way to quiet the noises made as Agent Topaz fought. Detective Nicholson had apparently heard that.

To Agent Ruby's horror, the halfling with the magical mirror that could see him during the planetary alignment rounded the corner. She was on the far end of the corridor and walking slowly, holding the mirror out and rotating every few paces, trying to find anything hidden. It was Agent Ruby, and he wasn't going to have Paris Beaufont ruin this for him again.

The halfling, who shouldn't be at Happily Ever After College at all, already foiled his plan with FriendNet. When he was Saint Valentine, he wouldn't only kick Paris out of school. He'd make her pay for ruining things.

Having anticipated that someone might intervene with his social media plan to bring down the love meter, Agent Ruby had already had the cell phone idea in the works. The current Saint Valentine supported technology and encouraged its use in matchmaking. When it was the downfall to relationships worldwide, the FGA board would have no choice but to fire the leader and replace him with Agent Ruby.

The fairy in the cell sputtered out his last breath as Agent Ruby tightened the makeshift noose around his neck, using magic. He let out a breath of relief, grateful he'd finished the job. Agent Topaz was gone, and it looked like a suicide. No one would question it. He'd be the one thought responsible for Agent Opal's death. Saint Valentine would let down his guard once more and not see it coming when the board booted him from office.

Feeling especially drained from the spell work, Agent Ruby lowered his silver ballpoint pen. All he had to do was sneak by Paris Beaufont, who made her way in his direction. He'd considered going the opposite way, but that's where Screaming Sasha was loose, and there would be more obstacles to overcome on that route.

Agent Ruby wasn't worried about walking by a worthless halfling who was playing detective. Once he was past her, then he'd be free, and this part of his plan would be complete. Then the issues with the phones would come to a head and everything else would fall perfectly into place.

Taking a quiet step forward, Agent Ruby plastered himself to the black wall. He had to get by the halfling with the magic mirror.

CHAPTER SIXTY-FIVE

"How much longer, squirrel?" Lunis rhythmically beat his wings to keep them hovering in one spot.

Faraday tapped the keys of the laptop several times, nothing happening to his horror. "I've encountered a problem with my computer. I think the altitude is affecting the system."

"Have you tried turning it off and back on?" Sophia asked, totally chill although they had red laser beams streaking by them on either side. Unfortunately, the dragonriders hadn't been able to shield them entirely, but so far none had hit them. It had made for a bumpy ride as Lunis tried to dodge attacks while staying in place. The laptop had bounced around a lot, and that could be affecting the hardware too, causing the problem.

"Interesting that the definition of insanity is doing the same thing over and over and expecting different results," Lunis mused. "However, not if you're restarting a computer, hoping to fix an issue."

"We're getting overrun here," Wilder said over the comms. "The drones figured out how to get their shields back up."

"Hearing this about the drones above us isn't the worst thing I've heard all day," Lunis began. "But it's definitely up there."

"Oh, man, Lunis," Evan groaned. "If these drones don't kill me, your jokes might."

"Don't get my hopes up," Lunis quipped.

"How much longer can you hold them off?" Sophia asked over the comms.

"We're taking a lot of damage," one of the Rogue Riders answered. "We can shield only for a little longer before we suffer a casualty."

"And shooting down the drones? Is that a possibility?" Sophia asked.

"Honestly, at this point, we're trying to distract them so they don't waylay the Rogue Riders," Wilder answered over the comms.

"Whoever created these things is smart and also on my hit list," Evan stated.

"Yeah, I've never seen magitech like this," Mark offered.

For the first time that day, Sophia gave Faraday an urgent look. "I can't lose a rider or a dragon. I'm sorry, but you have got one minute before we retreat."

The squirrel nodded frantically, doing something that as a scientist, he'd never done before—he prayed.

CHAPTER SIXTY-SIX

Screaming Sasha was proving to be quite the fighter. When King Rudolf kicked her, she rolled to the side but launched herself straight back at Lee.

The assassin baker, knowing that getting space from the fairy with assaulting vocals was crucial for survival, crab-walked down the hallway quickly but lost her coordination as Screaming Sasha drew in a deep breath.

Lee shot to her feet and ran backward several yards.

King Rudolf was going to have to do what he did best yet again and save the day. He crossed his arms and stood bravely in place.

"Hey, as the king of the fae and quite the influence in the fairy world, why don't I grant you a pardon," he offered.

Screaming Sasha spun around, and her beady eyes narrowed on Rudolf. "You'd do that?" she asked, not with her violent tone but still too loudly. This was one of those people who didn't understand personal volume and ruined all experiences with her noise pollution.

King Rudolf nodded, keeping his eyes on Screaming Sasha although he saw Lee quietly reaching for the baton she'd dropped earlier.

"Hey, Screaming Sasha!" a prisoner in a cell next to where Lee was kneeling yelled.

Rudolf's pulse quickened. The inmate was going to alert the ugly fairy to Lee unless he acted fast. "Of course I can do that. But you have to sign an agreement that states you won't use your gorgeous vocals to harm others anymore."

The woman tucked her head back, her many chins more prominent. There was a glimmer of mischief in her small eyes. "I will sign this agreement. Then I get freed?"

Lee was approaching soundlessly from behind Screaming Sasha, the baton raised in the air.

"Hey, Screaming Sasha!" the inmate called again.

"What!" the fairy yelled, spinning around.

Fortunately, Lee was right behind her and brought the baton across her head, knocking her out at once. Unfortunately, her scream blasted Lee straight on, sending her several yards backward, making her land hard on the concrete where she hit her head against the wall, passing out as well.

Rudolf threw his hands up and rolled his eyes. "Great! I had to save the day, and now I've got to save your life, Lee. You'll owe me a cookie for this."

CHAPTER SIXTY-SEVEN

Adrenaline beat in Paris' veins as she took each step down the dark jail hallway. The fact that she had the mirror in one hand and no weapon in the other did nothing to make her feel better. She comforted herself that the mirror was in her left hand and her right was strongest at punching.

Using the tiny compact to see the area around her was cumbersome to say the very least. It was a very small surface, and the darkness of the corridor didn't help.

"Hey, it's you!" a fairy in a neighboring cell called to her. "Why don't you come over here."

"Go hang yourself, Michelle," Paris grumbled, trying to stay focused as she revolved, trying to catch sight of anything unusual in the mirror.

"So you do remember that you're the one who landed me in this joint then?" the woman asked. She was a junkie fairy who Paris had caught stealing prescription medication from an elderly fairy couple.

"Your drug addiction and ruthless ways are what landed you in here." Paris continued her trek, her progress slow but steady. There couldn't be much time left in the hour of the perfect planetary alignment. She had to find out who let out Screaming Sasha—she owed that to Uncle John.

"Why don't you come closer and I'll show you ruthless," Michelle fired back.

"Would you shut up!" Paris yelled. "I'm bu—"

She froze. Her words cut off. Holding the mirror steady, she spied something in the reflection that she knew for a fact wasn't there when she looked down the hallway. Paris glanced over her shoulder, spying an empty dark hallway. Looking back at the mirror, she saw a very clear image that chilled her blood.

Standing only a few feet behind her was Agent Ruby, his silver ballpoint pen in his hands, pointed straight at her.

CHAPTER SIXTY-EIGHT

Maybe it was praying or focusing or science, but Faraday was suddenly able to hone in on the broadcasting signal from the satellite.

"I only need to run the program," he said in a rush, bouncing up and down on the dragon's back as Lunis tried to avoid laser beams streaking by them.

"And how long will that take?" Sophia asked urgently.

Never before had a progress bar on a computer brought so much tension to Faraday's chest. "Hopefully only ten to twenty seconds."

"That's about as long as we can hold on," Evan said over the comms.

"I'm never letting you live it down that you got bested by some tiny drones," Sophia teased, again surprising Faraday with how casual she could be during a battle.

"Do it," Evan chirped. "These aren't normal drones. Once we're better prepared, I'm coming back and taking all these jerks down. Then I'm finding their maker and employing his services."

"Or hers," Faraday said, thinking of the magitech scientist, Alicia—although she wasn't the maker of these drones.

"Our formation is hosed," a Rogue Rider said. "We can't hold much longer."

Sophia stared at Faraday. But it was the *ding* of his computer that told them the mission was over.

"The signal is down!" Faraday exclaimed. "Cell phones will no longer be addictive."

"Well, unless you're Evan and constantly checking his Instagram for new 'likes,'" Wilder teased over the comms.

"Who doesn't like a good dopamine hit," Evan cheered.

"Okay, time to retreat," Sophia ordered, pulling on Lunis' reins, steering him back toward the Earth's surface. "Fall out of formation."

"Kick it into jet mode, team," Wilder encouraged. "Let's outrace these guys."

Sophia threw up a portal in the distance, and they slipped through it to safety. The other dragonriders did something similar when they were a safe distance from the drones.

Faraday exhaled, feeling like he'd held his breath the entire time. But he'd done it—he'd finally done something of great significance. Faraday, the squirrel, had helped to restore love.

CHAPTER SIXTY-NINE

"It was you," Paris muttered, chilled by the fact that Agent Ruby was standing behind her, but she couldn't see him with her eyes, only in the surface of the mirror.

There was something wrong with the fairy—well, besides that he was evil, and she suspected he was behind Agent Opal's death as well as the FriendNet debacle.

It was hard to tell in the darkened corridor and with Agent Ruby's black bowler hat obscuring his face, but he appeared paler than Paris remembered. Sweat was also pouring down his face, making him look like he'd run a marathon.

"Yes, it was me," he snarled. To her surprise, he didn't attack her with magic although he was still pointing the silver ballpoint pen with the red heart-shaped ruby on its end at her.

Paris would have to stall because she didn't know how to attack Agent Ruby with her back toward him. If she turned, getting him in the mirror was going to be difficult. No, she needed to buy some time while she figured out the best approach.

"You let out Screaming Sasha," Paris stated. "But why? Who is she to you?"

A wicked grin spread on his face, and he shook his head. "You're such a naïve and unmannered waste of space."

"I don't happen to like you much either," Paris remarked, trying to memorize where he was behind her. That way she could throw a combat spell at him, but she couldn't miss. She couldn't stall much longer. Now that she was studying him, Agent Ruby looked depleted, as if he'd used a great store of magic. His hand with the silver ballpoint pen shook. He didn't have much magic right now, but with each passing moment, he might be recuperating.

"Well, now I'll be able to prove that you were behind FriendNet and who knows what else," Paris remarked, sifting through her options.

The cold chuckle that fell from his mouth was devoid of any joy. "No one is going to believe a halfling with demon blood over an agent at FGA. You are and will always be out of my league."

"You don't get it," Paris remarked. "You've been caught. Now tell me, why did you let Screaming Sasha out of her cell."

"I don't have time for this," Agent Ruby muttered angrily.

Paris realized that he was right. The planetary alignment was almost over. Then she'd be able to see him clearly without the mirror, and the security wards would be back up at the FLEA jail.

But something else occurred to her then. Screaming Sasha's cell was on the western side of the jail. So what was Agent Ruby doing on the far eastern side?

Paris' eyes flickered down the corridor, something occurring to her suddenly. "You're here to release Agent Topaz? Of course," she said with a gasp. "You two were working together to take out Saint Valentine."

"We're done here." He fired, flicking the tip of his silver ballpoint pen at Paris. A stream of magic wobbled out the tip and sadly fell to the floor without enough force to hit or hurt with a combat spell. However, it threw Paris into action. She spun and threw up her hand, pointing it where she'd seen Agent Ruby in the mirror. Her combat spell flew from her hand, but the sound of an assault didn't follow. He must have moved.

Paris shot to the side, holding up the mirror, searching for the invisible man's position. To her horror, she realized he was right next to her. His fist smashed against her face, sending her back against the concrete wall. The mirror flew from her hand, crashing to the floor and shattering at once.

As Paris fell, she made one last-ditch effort to catch the invisible man, launching herself forward and reaching. Her hand grabbed his leg, and he tumbled forward, falling on the concrete floor. Something else sounded like it broke. Maybe the silver ballpoint pen in his hand. However, Agent Ruby was strong and used his invisibility to his advantage. He kicked hard, his shoe connecting with Paris' head.

He jerked out of her grasp, and she heard the sound of running. Paris shot to her feet, looking for any of the shattered mirror pieces but they were all too small to be of use. Without that, it would be impossible to catch him. Plus, she had to stop Agent Topaz. That's why she made the impromptu decision and decided to divide their efforts.

"Uncle John!" she yelled. "It's Agent Ruby. He's running for the exit now! Stop him!"

Then Paris turned, racing toward Agent Topaz's cell, hoping it wasn't too late to stop both agents from getting away.

CHAPTER SEVENTY

Detective John Nicholson barely made out Paris' words echoing down the corridor. He stood squarely in the entrance to the FLEA jail. Although John didn't have magic, he was as strong as he'd been in his youth, thanks to being a Mortal Seven. However, not being able to see his enemy would prove to be a problem.

He heard the running footsteps. Holding up his hand, John narrowed his eyes, willing himself to see anything hidden by the planetary alignment. "Stop! You're not getting out of here!"

The sound of a humorless laugh from a disembodied figure was chilling. "You can't stop me."

John held up his hand, sensing where the voice was coming from. He knew how to fight, but better than that, he understood how to out-bluff, and that was strategy—a much smarter approach than using force. He pointed the palm of his hand where the voice came from, the way he had seen magical races do when about to use a spell. "Stop, or I'll throw a stunning spell at you."

Agent Ruby laughed again, sounding satisfied. "We both know that you're not a fairy. The planetary alignment makes things that aren't supposed to be there known, and your wings are fake. That's quite obvious now. You're a mortal and have no magic."

Oh, hell. John braced himself in the doorway. He'd have to rely on his brute strength after all. However, the blast that hit him took him by surprise, knocking him to the side, away from the exit.

CHAPTER SEVENTY-ONE

What Paris found when she raced to Agent Topaz's jail cell was not what she expected. She thought she'd find him gone. She anticipated that the cell would be open. However, what she didn't think she'd discover was Agent Topaz hanging in his jail cell—the door locked.

However, she knew with certainty that Agent Ruby had killed him.

Once again, proving this was going to be the challenge. That man was excellent at covering his tracks. He'd blamed everything on Agent Topaz, and now he'd killed the one person who could rat him out.

Paris had to find a way to expose him. Saint Valentine had to know that his agent was double-crossing him, trying to murder him, sabotage him, and doing anything and everything it took to cover his tracks.

Turning away from the sickly sight of the dead man hanging from his jail cell by his bedsheets, Paris tried to process. Seeing the dead fairy had done something raw to her. She knew she should run to the entrance to help Uncle John. That she should do anything to help, but suddenly she felt sick to her stomach.

That's when she saw it—the one thing that she needed all along to connect Agent Ruby to the crimes even if he got away that night. Even if he had an excuse. No matter what, she had what she needed to ensure he went down for his crimes. Or at least into hiding. Then she'd track him down and get him in his sleep. No matter what, Agent Ruby was going to pay.

CHAPTER SEVENTY-TWO

All hopes that Uncle John had stopped Agent Ruby died when she rushed to the entrance of the FLEA jail to find her uncle sprawled beside the open door. He was out cold, and there was a nasty welt on his head from a spell. However, he was breathing, and for that, Paris was grateful.

The door to the jail was open, and she didn't have to guess that the fairy had enough magic to get past a mortal. It hadn't worked on Paris because of her halfling blood, but mortals were always more susceptible to magic, even the small bits that Agent Ruby had in his reserves.

"Uncle John." Paris knelt and cradled his head, feeling for his pulse. It was strong. There was no sign of Agent Ruby through the door and Paris was certain that the invisible fairy had gotten away by this time. It had been several minutes since he'd fled from her.

Uncle John bolted upright with a start and looked around, suddenly on guard and ready to fight. He spun and at the sight of Paris he seemed confused. Then he deflated.

"Oh, Pare...I screwed up...I let him get away..."

Paris looked him over, wanting to dismiss his worries as soon as she alleviated her concerns about his safety. "How do you feel? Are you okay?"

Uncle John clapped his hand to his chest and felt around for a moment as if he might have lost something. Then he shook his head. "I'm fine. I got knocked out, but aside from a headache, I'm fine."

She nodded. "That's normal. He hit you with a stunning spell. There was nothing you could do. Agent Ruby was invisible, motivated, and had magic. He was going to do whatever he needed to get away before we caught him."

Her uncle looked around. "What did he come here for? Was he trying to get Screaming Sasha out?"

She shook her head, still trying to piece it together, but sure she understood at this point. "No, I think that was a diversion."

"For what?" he asked as she stood, extended a hand for him, and helped him to his feet.

"So he could murder Agent Topaz."

Uncle John's eyes went wide. "Agent Topaz is dead?"

She nodded, trying to erase the sight from her memory. "Yeah, and that's where I met Agent Ruby. I bet his fellow agent was the only one who could provide evidence to incriminate him for FriendNet or Agent Opal's murder."

"Which explains why Agent Topaz hadn't been offering any information before his trial," Uncle John stated.

"Yes, so I think that Agent Ruby used the planetary alignment as his opportunity to take out the one person who could connect him to the murder and FriendNet," Paris explained.

Uncle John deflated. "But I didn't ID him. You probably couldn't …"

"In the mirror," Paris offered.

"Unfortunately, that won't hold up in a court of law." Uncle John sounded defeated. "It looks like once again, we don't have any way to connect Agent Ruby to the crimes he's committed, even after another death."

"Well," Paris drew out the word. "I found something at the scene of Agent Topaz's murder that could only belong to one person. Not only can it only belong to Agent Ruby, but it will have the remnants of his magic all over it."

Uncle John arched a curious eyebrow at her. She had his attention.

Paris held up her hand and opened her fingers to reveal the heart-shaped ruby. It must have broken off his silver ballpoint pen when she tripped him. And he'd left it behind—the one thing that would connect him to the jail, the murder, to all the criminal activity.

A victorious laugh popped out of Uncle John's mouth. "Ha! That couldn't be more perfect, Pare. This will show all the spells that Agent Ruby has done in the last several months. That's the way FGA keeps accountability. The way we linked Agent Topaz to the murder of Agent Opal."

"Which I believe Agent Ruby stole his pocket watch to perform that poisoning spell," Paris remarked.

Uncle John nodded and took the red heart-shaped ruby from her. "I think your instincts are as good as a detective's. Always trust them, Pare. You know what you're doing."

CHAPTER SEVENTY-THREE

Paris and Uncle John rushed down the dark corridor, following the sounds of moans. They came from Lee and King Rudolf, who were sitting with their backs against the concrete wall opposite the cells.

Paris glanced around, grateful to find all the prisoners locked up—Screaming Sasha was in her cell once more.

She looked the two over, thinking they appeared fine, although both cradled their heads. "Are you two all right? What happened to you?"

Lee pointed at Screaming Sasha, who thankfully couldn't scream inside her magic-proofed cell. "She knocked me out...twice."

King Rudolf pointed at Lee. "And she clocked me...once...I think."

"Why did you do that?" Paris asked the assassin baker.

"He was healing me from the assault that evil witch did to me," Lee began. "But it was so nice and loving that I awoke with a start and knocked him out."

King Rudolf shrugged. "What can I say. I have a gentle touch."

"So you two are okay?" Uncle John helped Lee up first, then King Rudolf.

"I need a drink," Lee said.

"I need ten," the fae stated.

"But yeah, we got that evil fairy back away." Lee shook her head and narrowed her eyes at Screaming Sasha. "I can't believe someone wanted that loudmouth out."

"I think they let her out as a diversion," Paris began as the foursome walked out of the jail. "We have quite the story to tell you all now that the planetary alignment is over."

"I have to hear this story," King Rudolf sang. "Let's get some drinks."

"And some pizza," Lee added.

"And a painkiller." Uncle John rubbed his head.

Paris pressed her hand to the side of her head where Agent Ruby had punched her, finally feeling it throb. "Yeah. Then we're going to figure out how to take down a very evil fairy who needs to be brought to justice."

CHAPTER SEVENTY-FOUR

"I can't say I'm surprised," Saint Valentine said, his ornately silver cane in one hand as he rested crossed-legged in an armchair in Headmistress Willow Starr's office at Happily Ever After College.

"One of your agents," Willow repeated, offended. "You're not surprised?"

"Well, before we suspected Agent Topaz," Saint Valentine said in his distinguished voice. "I know better than most that there are many at FGA who don't like my ways."

"But to murder?" Willow questioned.

"You knew before that someone was trying to murder me," Saint Valentine stated. "Once someone starts down that path, it gets easier to keep going. So Agent Ruby was trying to cover his tracks."

"It sounds like you're making excuses for him." Willow was visibly offended as she pressed a hand to her chest.

Saint Valentine pointed at the side of his head. "I know how people think and can follow their path. Agent Ruby, like many, doesn't like how I'm conducting my administration. He's desperate to do anything to stop me. As such, he believes that his actions are warranted. As he gets deeper, so do the lengths he'll go to." The man with a polished appearance and calm expression shrugged with regret. "I fear that he's gotten himself so deep that there's no coming back."

"Well, I hope not," Willow said shrilly. "He's murdered…twice."

"I realize that," Saint Valentine stated calmly. "But I always wish salvation for evildoers, if not for their souls."

Mae Ling nodded. "I fear that Ruby must be stopped by any means necessary rather than reasoned with at this point."

"I'm afraid so." Saint Valentine looked thoughtfully at Paris. "But I'm grateful that we know who we're looking for, rather than believing we had caught our criminal. Although I'm sorry that Agent Topaz suffered the price for this."

Paris glanced at the heart-shaped ruby sitting on the headmistress' desk. "Me too. I hope I can help however you like."

Saint Valentine's warm chuckle filled the office. "You learned who the man was who tried to murder me. Stopped his operation to disrupt the love meter via cell phones. And pretty much risked your life and that of your friends to do so." He tilted his head, looking at Paris with a deep penetrating gaze. "You know, my instinct tells me that you're going places here at FGA and not only as a fairy godmother. Few act with the same courage and tenacity as you."

Paris suddenly felt fidgety, not knowing what to do with her hands. She smiled awkwardly. "I have my friend Faraday to thank for fixing the signal with the cell phones. And my Aunt Sophia Beaufont."

He laughed again. "Oh, I've met Sophia. She's a woman after my own heart and will be getting a special box of chocolates from me in thanks. It seems I owe the Beaufonts many thank yous."

"So Agent Ruby," Willow began, her voice full of tension. She'd seemed very on edge since the beginning of the meeting. This kind of thing was definitely outside her wheelhouse. "What will you do now, Saint Valentine?"

"Well, we're on the lookout for him, of course," Saint Valentine began, rising with the use of his cane. "FLEA is on high alert as well as the House of Fourteen and other organizations. I dare say, if that fairy shows his face anywhere, someone will see it."

"We shouldn't underestimate him," Mae Ling interjected with an air of authority.

Saint Valentine nodded. "He's conspired to great lengths to bring me down and take my position. Ruby is a good opponent, but I have the best around me." He proudly looked at the love meter on the wall of the headmistress' office wall, which had recovered already after Faraday had stopped the signal broadcasting to cell phones to make them addictive. "We do great work when we work together. Imagine what we can do when we clean house and work toward a mission united."

Headmistress Starr rose, smiling. "That's my main goal, Saint Valentine."

"Mine too," Mae Ling stated, remaining seated.

"And mine." Paris stood with a slight bow, surprising herself.

Saint Valentine bowed to her with a smile. "I have a renewed sense of hope that I haven't had in a long time that we can reach that goal together. First, let us take care of those who stand in our path. Then let's forge ahead together, creating love for all."

Paris smiled, watching as Saint Valentine left, his grace and charisma like pixie dust wafting in the air behind him.

CHAPTER SEVENTY-FIVE

Paris had never been so excited in her entire life. Growing up by herself with Uncle John in a small apartment on Roya Lane, they'd shared a simple life. Holidays had been small—only the two of them. She had liked them, and he'd always made them special. But still, they'd been small.

Paris didn't know what she'd been missing, maybe because Papa Creola had spelled her. But also because she didn't know any different. Uncle John's love had always felt like enough. However, Paris didn't know how much bigger her life could be. She was learning that.

"Mom, are you ready?" Paris asked her mother, standing next to her in the basement of the Fantastical Armory.

Liv glanced up at her, smoothing down her black top that looked much like the one Paris always wore. "Do I look ready? Should I mess up my hair? It doesn't look brushed, does it?"

Paris laughed. "You have my same aversion to brushing your hair."

"It's inherited." Stefan threaded his arm through his wife's.

"I think it's going to be weirder for all of them, more than us," Liv stated.

"No," Stefan argued. "It's going to be perfect. Everything with you is always perfect. You never realize it because you're...well, you."

"That's one of the most ridiculous things you've ever said, Stefan Ludwig." Liv shook her head at her husband.

He gave her a challenging look. "What's the most ridiculous thing I've ever said?"

"I do. It's also the best thing."

He kissed her before looking at Paris. "Are you ready?"

She nodded, not sure why it should matter. This was her world. It was only her parents that were joining it, although she'd only recently entered it too. They were all coming together after fifteen years apart.

Right on cue, the portal shimmered in front of them, and the three stepped through it to a place that was exactly like the apartment where they'd been—but this one was the real place. The one where Liv and Stefan had raised Paris. The one her parents had shared before. The one in Los Angeles above Uncle John's electronics repair shop.

Paris was finally home, but more importantly, with her parents.

Even better was that all their friends were there too.

CHAPTER SEVENTY-SIX

The cheers of people around Paris, Liv, and Stefan were all-encompassing when they stepped through the portal to the apartment in West Hollywood.

There wasn't a face that Paris didn't recognize or wasn't full of love and smiles. Arms reached in to grab Liv and Stefan, holding them in tightly, wanting to hug them to know they were real. To feel them. To know they were real and finally back.

Many grabbed for Paris too, and she didn't know some of the faces. A woman with a thoughtful smile and brown hair and eyes introduced herself as her Aunt Raina. Another said that she was a healer by the name of Hester. Everyone was happy, and before long, the apartment was full of laughter.

"I told you that if you didn't dump that man, he'd take you away from your friends and family," King Rudolf said after finally releasing Liv once she begged for a solid minute.

Liv pointed at Stefan and shook her head. "He didn't steal me away. It was the Deathly Shadow."

"That's what he wants you to believe." Rudolf shook his head. He pointed at Stefan. "I've got your number, Evil Villain."

Paris' father waved casually at the fae. "Good to see you too, Ru."

The king of the fae shook his head. "Don't suck up to me, demon lover."

"Hunter," Liv corrected. "He hunts demons. Not loves them."

"Enough about him." Rudolf clung to Liv's hand. "We have to start up our weekly bowling league. Oh! And poker tournaments. I've had t-shirts made, although you look like you've put on weight in the last fifteen years. I'll get a bigger size for you."

Liv laughed, not at all seeming put off by the fae—probably used to him. "I wasn't gone fifteen years, remember. That's why I haven't aged. And you apparently didn't either."

Rudolf leaned forward. "I've been dipping into a secret stash of Heals Pills. A high-dose formula. Oh, and also, I'm not a gross magician."

"Thanks, I am one," Liv stated blandly. "We didn't have a poker game or a bowling league, and we're starting one never. I'm looking forward to starting back as a Warrior full time."

"We're looking forward to having you," Raina said. She was a Councilor for the House of Fourteen and Paris' aunt on her father's side.

"Things will benefit from your strategic approach," Hester DeVries stated.

"Although we've managed in your absence, there's something about the way that Liv and Stefan took care of things," Clark said, raising a champagne flute into the air. "Cheers to peace hopefully reigning in the magical world once more."

"And demons put to rest," Raina stated, looking fondly at her brother.

"And magical communities finding peaceful solutions again," a deep voice said from the door.

All turned to find a giant standing there.

Liv's face was suddenly full of shock and awe. She pressed her wine glass into her husband's hand and pushed past the crowd, making her way to the man with curly brown hair and tender green eyes standing in the doorway.

Paris knew from hearing her parent's stories that Rory Laurens was Liv's first magical friend when she came back as a magician after her parent's death, when she joined the House of Fourteen.

Rory, the giant, had treated her coldly at first, but Liv had said the magic of a giant was when they first warmed to a person. It meant something more than when others showed affection. Giants didn't give away love, compliments, or smiles easily. So their affection somehow meant more.

That's why tears prickled at Paris' eyes when her mother ran for the doorway, jumped into the air, and threw her arms around Rory's neck. The giant picked her up and whirled her around like a little doll, his face wide with a smile.

When Rory Laurens set Liv down, he was still grinning at the Warrior for the House of Fourteen. "I've missed you every single day that you've been gone, Liv Beaufont. I'm so happy that you're back. Hopefully, for me and this world, you're back for good."

CHAPTER SEVENTY-SEVEN

"Do you think it makes me look fat?" Faraday looked in the mirror on the vanity in Paris' room.

She nearly doubled over from laughter. "I think you'll need to do some ab exercises to wear it."

Saint Valentine had given Faraday a medallion with a beautiful symbol of honor for his work fixing the cell phone problem. It was on a lovely velvet ribbon and attached to a talisman with Saint Valentine's unique seal on it and the words, "For Noble Service and Courage."

The metal was draped over the squirrel's neck but hung down low and would drag if Faraday tried to move. "Well, I might wear it at fancy events," he said.

Paris laughed. "What fancy events? All those dinner parties you attend?"

"Who knows," he said smugly. "I made friends with dragons."

"Who tell fart jokes," Paris replied, so happy for her friend. "I'm sure that in the future, you'll have lots of opportunities to show off your medal. You're a big deal here at the college and FGA. Not only did you gain favor with fixing everyone's phones, but then after they were all addicted to them, you fixed them."

Faraday rolled his eyes, pulled off the medal, and draped it carefully around the side of the vanity. "I didn't know when I fixed phones that there was going to be a signal creating an addiction to mobile devices."

"Without you, we wouldn't have been able to fix it." Paris pulled back her bed covers and slid into her sheets, feeling like she hadn't slept in a month…and she might not have rested properly in all that time. There had always been so much excitement and danger and things to think about for her to sleep. It wasn't like that was going to change now though.

"So Agent Ruby is still at large." Faraday hopped over to his sock drawer, seemingly having read her mind about how things were still demanding her attention.

"I don't think we call him Agent Ruby anymore," Paris offered, pulling her covers up to her chest.

"Jerk-Ruby," Faraday stated.

"I like it." Paris laughed. "And yes, I think we haven't seen the last of him yet. If Saint Valentine is right, he'll be more vengeful than before. He'll want revenge against me for blowing his cover. Once FGA found out about him because of the ruby he left behind at the FLEA jail, they went to his home, but he'd already fled, knowing that he'd blown his cover. Anyway, Saint Valentine thinks he'll go off his rocker now since he'd already committed murder."

"Sounds like we better rest up." Faraday yawned and rustled around in his drawer, getting comfortable.

Paris snapped her fingers, shutting off her lamp beside her bed, casting them in soft darkness. "Yes, and we can wake up tomorrow and stop the bad guys interfering with love and help the good guys trying to assist love."

"And in between," Faraday added, "maybe we can find something special for us."

Paris closed her eyes, a smile on her face and in her heart. Content in all senses of the word. "I think that sounds lovely. Good night, Faraday. Thanks for saving the world."

"You're welcome." Faraday sounded close to falling asleep. "It's people like you who make it worth it."

Thank you a ton for reading! Your support means more than I can ever say. Ever. But I will try. Thank you.

Should I start these author notes with telling you how I nearly burned down my house on purpose or how I cried in front of two unassuming pest control guys?

I'll start with the first one.

I hit the deadline on this book yet again, but not without peril. I almost thought I was going to have to tell Mike that I was going to miss the deadline because my COVID kitten (as I affectionately call her), also known as Ainsley, wanted to play fetch...nonstop.

Yes, I named her after the housekeeper from the Sophia Beaufont series, although she doesn't have red hair and probably can't shapeshift...probably... Anyway, we got Ains in September when I kept trekking off to Scotland and my other cat would get lonely when I left him for long stretches.

Ainsley has never known a life where Lydia, my daughter, goes to school, since she's homeschooled. Besides my week long trips to Scotland, I'm home most of the time as a reclusive writer. So needless to say, COVID kitten is codependent as hell. I can't even go to the bathroom without her freaking out. Wait, this was supposed to be a story about how I almost burned down my house in order to start anew. I'll get back on the rails.

Anyway, so the cat I named after a character from my own book, as I tend to do, loves to play fetch. She confiscated pipe cleaners from Lydia's room from some art project she'd done (not because she smokes a pipe). The cat wads them up into balls and likes for us to throw them and three seconds later Ains brings them back and barks at us like a freaking dog to throw it again. And this goes on for hours…

So I'm trying to hit this deadline but COVID kitten is like, "play fetch!" And I'm usually okay with getting distracted, so I kept indulging her as the deadline got closer.

I told Lydia at one point, "I might have to call Michael and tell him I can't get the book done on time because I'm throwing pipe cleaners for my kitten."

So one sunny day, I turn from my office chair to throw the pipe cleaner since the cat is barking at me to play. To my horror, I find the grossest beast just stomping across my office floor. It was a tiny bug, but mighty. And it had claws like a scorpion and too many legs and these protruding eyes and again, it was stomping in my direction. So *I* stomped on it…after taking a video and some pictures for Instagram (of course). It didn't die easily, but it did die. Then I flushed the monster.

I promptly walked down stairs and told Lydia to pack up and we were moving out. I was certain we had scorpions in the house. Baby scorpions which would grow into adult ones.

Side note, don't go look up baby scorpions on the internet unless you want to loose your lunch.

My sweet child was like, "WHAT?" I showed her the video. I told her all was safe in the house but that we were burning it down to be safe and that we'd start again somewhere else.

She giggled and said, "Can I resume listening to my audio book?"

Side note #2. My daughter is on book 10 of a dragon series and it's not mine…I really think I should ground her for this.

Anyway, I called the exterminator, which I've never done. When I first moved in, the neighbors called this the witch's house because I refused to use chemicals to get rid of the ants. Instead I had chalk lines and essential oils sprayed around the perimeter. Guess how well that worked…

But scorpions, well hell to the no. Those little beasts were leaving the house…Or I was.

So I called the pest control people and they said they'd show up sometime in the morning the next day. I was like great, I'll meanwhile hover around the house instead of touch the floor. But I quickly forgot about the demons who could be living in the shadows of my home because I had a book to write.

The next morning, I realized I was procrastinating writing a certain chapter. I realize those kinds of things when I start telling Lydia we need to organize the linen closets or I decide to randomly message my accountant to see how he's doing.

Why was I putting off this chapter? Because it was going to be an emotional beating. It was the one where Liv, Clark and Sophia are reunited after 15 years. The key for me was nailing the emotion which would be a bit lopsided. It had been 15 years since Clark and Sophia had seen Liv. But for her, it had only been a week or so. I needed to really feel the strangeness of the situation. The anticipation. Liv's empathy for the loss her siblings were feeling. The regrets of lost years and time.

So I'm getting into the scene and I start balling. Like full on mascara running down my face and puffy cheeks. And I can't stop. Once I opened the flood gates of empathy, there was no closing those babies. You all know what happened next, right?

Knock. Knock.

The exterminators had arrived and I couldn't stop crying.

Oh, universe, you really have a lot of fun when it comes to me, don't you?

I had to answer the door because sending my nine-year old to deal with pest control isn't something I've graduated to yet. So I answered the door, my face red from crying and did what anyone would do. I explained that I'm a fiction writer and yes, I was just crying because I was writing an emotional chapter.

The guy was like, "Most women would be crying because of the scorpion…"

I'd entirely forgotten about that revolting beasts.

The poor pest control really didn't know what to do with me at that point. So I just told them I'd be inside writing about a magician who'd been trapped in another dimension and had returned after 15 years. They were like, "Cool…We'll spray the property."

Turns out that it was a jumping spider who apparently bite and like to impersonate scorpions but aren't venomous. Lydia was like, that should make you feel better that it was a jumping spider. To which I responded, "Did you miss the part where it jumps!?"

I really don't mind spiders and usually don't even mess with cobwebs. I've been known to name the daddy long legs who live in the bathroom. However, I draw the line at clawed scorpion impersonators who can freaking launch themselves into the air. Thankfully the place is spider-proofed for a bit. And thankfully for the exterminators, they don't have to deal with my emotional ass for a while.

Okay, well, that should give MA a novella to pretend to have read and reply to. Bird Killer, tell the group about the pest you've killed.

Much love and Peace,
Tiny Ninja

Thank you for both reading this story and these author notes in the back!

I'm going to consider changing my name from bird-killer to author-squasher if she keeps this up.

Last year (in keeping with the theme), we moved to a house from a condo on the 25th floor. One thing you do not (generally) need to worry about in a condo so high up, are bugs.

The little pests have to work through 24 floors of insecticide to make it to my home.

This is where the move came in to upset my little apple cart. Seems that purchasing a home that has been without a tenant for about nine months (although sprayed outside) is still not fully protected.

While we live in a desert, it's not like we don't have insects (ants, spiders, SCORPIONS… etc. etc.)

My wife is all about kicking ass…except those of frogs and scorpions. She is a bit focused on those things.

Oh, and lizards. HATES them with a passion.

"But…lizards eat insects." I'll tell her. She looks at me as if I'm about to be the one with her size six and a half upside my head.

So, she sees a dead scorpion outside a few months back. Guess who has to purchase these blacklight flashlights to show scorpions in your house? (Apparently, blacklight shines off of scorpions.)

The flashlights have sat dormant around the house for the most part. I shined them a few times, found nothing… mostly forgot about them.

The other night, I come downstairs and what do I see in the entryway?

A flattened scorpion. This isn't going to go well - for me, that is. The scorpion had already had its bad hair day.

Sure enough, my lovely wife pointed out that she left the ex-Arachnida to show me that she was right about scorpions coming in the house. I, perhaps, had not expected the little A-holes to be around, and coming into the house if they were around.

I dutifully got on the phone with our pest control company and called to get an inside spray setup post-haste.

Now, I start looking into the damned corners of the restrooms in the middle of the night.

Oh, and I put my shoes out in the garage up on the little two-step ladder. Not that I'm phobic, but I am not having a sudden sting occur when I put on my shoes.

Great… Now this story will be in a book for historical purposes.

Have a great week or weekend, whatever works for your time of week!

Ad Aeternitatem,

Michael Anderle

ACKNOWLEDGMENTS
SARAH NOFFKE

I have so many people to thank who make this all possible. Firstly, thanks to Mike, who really pushes me to be a better writer, coming up with the best ideas, not just the really good ones. We work together pretty well, I'd say. I wonder what he'd say… Anyway, MA gave me the opportunity to write with LBMPN a few years ago and it's been life changing. He's very supportive and really cares. Thanks Bird Killer.

A huge thank you to the LBMPN team who work tirelessly so that I have less stress. Thanks to Steve and Kelly for making my life easier and being on top of everything. Thanks to Tracey and Lynne for fixing all my editing mistakes. A big thank you to the JIT team whose feedback at the 11th hour before publishing is invaluable. Thank you to my alpha readers Juergen and Martin. Thank you to everyone who makes getting the books to the reader possible. I really can't do this without you. And you make it so much more fun.

Thank you to my daughter, Lydia, who inspires my stories over and over again. She's my muse and we are always discussing story. She's an avid reader and listens to the Liv Beaufont series at night and reads the Sophia Beaufont books with me before bed. She also reads other authors, which I guess is okay. But my point is that she's supportive of me in so many ways. I need to stay immersed in this universe and remember all the details. There are 12 book in each series so there's a lot to remember. And Lydia loves my stories and then also supports me by listening and reading them so I can keep crafting. But also, she puts up with me when I go all psycho pants during a big crunch of a deadline. I will be the first to admit that I'm pretty intense a day or two before a book is due. And she always just smiles and says, "Mommy, you can do it."

Thank you to my family, the Scotsman and all my friends. You all are always so supportive of me and for that, I'm infinitely grateful. I really couldn't do this without the encouragement of those I love. On the really tough writing days, the Scotsman points out all the things that I don't see, like my dedication to the craft or how much readers are enjoying the books. I don't know what I did to have the most loving and thoughtful people in the world in my corner, but I'm going to do everything to keep them and hopefully keep making them proud.

And finally, thank you to you the reader. Without you I wouldn't be able to do what I love. Your support means so much to me and my family. Thank you from the bottom of my heart.

Love,
Tiny Ninja

Sarah Noffke writes YA and NA science fiction, fantasy, paranormal and urban fantasy. In addition to being an author, she is a mother, podcaster and professor. Noffke holds a Masters of Management and teaches college business/writing courses. Most of her students have no idea that she toils away her hours crafting fictional characters. www.sarahnoffke.com

Check out other work by Sarah author here.

Ghost Squadron:

Formation #1:

Kill the bad guys. Save the Galaxy. All in a hard day's work.

After ten years of wandering the outer rim of the galaxy, Eddie Teach is a man without a purpose. He was one of the toughest pilots in the Federation, but now he's just a regular guy, getting into bar fights and making a difference wherever he can. It's not the same as flying a ship and saving colonies, but it'll have to do.

That is, until General Lance Reynolds tracks Eddie down and offers him a job. There are bad people out there, plotting terrible things, killing innocent people, and destroying entire colonies. **Someone has to stop them.**

Eddie, along with the genetically-enhanced combat pilot Julianna Fregin and her trusty E.I. named Pip, must recruit a diverse team of specialists, both human and alien. They'll need to master their new Q-Ship, one of the most powerful strike ships ever constructed. And finally, they'll have to stop a faceless enemy so powerful, it threatens to destroy the entire Federation.

All in a day's work, right?

Experience this exciting military sci-fi saga and the latest addition to the expanded Kurtherian Gambit Universe. If you're a fan of Mass Effect, Firefly, or Star Wars, you'll love this riveting new space opera.

NOTE: If cursing is a problem, then this might not be for you.

Check out the entire series here.

The Precious Galaxy Series:

Corruption #1

A new evil lurks in the darkness.

After an explosion, the crew of a battlecruiser mysteriously disappears.

Bailey and Lewis, complete strangers, find themselves suddenly onboard the damaged ship. Lewis hasn't worked a case in years, not since the final one broke his spirit and his bank account. The last thing Bailey remembers is preparing to take down a fugitive on Onyx Station.

Mysteries are harder to solve when there's no evidence left behind.

Bailey and Lewis don't know how they got onboard *Ricky Bobby* or why. However, they quickly learn that whatever was responsible for the explosion and disappearance of the crew is still on the ship.

Monsters are real and what this one can do changes everything.

The new team bands together to discover what happened and how to fight the monster lurking in the bottom of the battlecruiser.

Will they find the missing crew? Or will the monster end them all?

The Soul Stone Mage Series:

House of Enchanted #1:

The Kingdom of Virgo has lived in peace for thousands of years...until now.

The humans from Terran have always been real assholes to the witches of Virgo. Now a silent war is brewing, and the timing couldn't be worse. Princess Azure will soon be crowned queen of the Kingdom of Virgo.

In the Dark Forest a powerful potion-maker has been murdered.

Charmsgood was the only wizard who could stop a deadly virus plaguing Virgo. He also knew about the devastation the people from Terran had done to the forest.

Azure must protect her people. Mend the Dark Forest. Create alliances with savage beasts. No biggie, right?

But on coronation day everything changes. Princess Azure isn't who she thought she was and that's a big freaking problem.

Welcome to The Revelations of Oriceran. Check out the entire series here.

The Lucidites Series:

Awoken, #1:

Around the world humans are hallucinating after sleepless nights.

In a sterile, underground institute the forecasters keep reporting the same events.

And in the backwoods of Texas, a sixteen-year-old girl is about to be caught up in a fierce, ethereal battle.

Meet Roya Stark. She drowns every night in her dreams, spends her hours reading classic literature to avoid her family's ridicule, and is prone to premonitions—which are becoming more frequent. And now her dreams are filled with strangers offering to reveal what she has always wanted to know: Who is she? That's the question that haunts her, and she's about to find out. But will Roya live to regret learning the truth?

Stunned, #2

Revived, #3

The Reverians Series:

Defects, #1:

In the happy, clean community of Austin Valley, everything appears to be perfect. Seventeen-year-old Em Fuller, however, fears something is askew. Em is one of the new generation of Dream Travelers. For some reason, the gods have not seen fit to gift all of them with their expected special abilities. Em is a Defect—one of the unfortunate Dream Travelers not gifted with a psychic power. Desperate to do whatever it takes to earn her gift, she endures painful daily injections along with commands from her overbearing, loveless father. One of the few bright spots in her life is the return of a friend she had thought dead—but with his return comes the knowledge of a shocking, unforgivable truth. The society Em thought was protecting her has actually been betraying her, but she has no idea how to break away from its authority without hurting everyone she loves.

Rebels, #2

Warriors, #3

Vagabond Circus Series:

Suspended, #1:

When a stranger joins the cast of Vagabond Circus—a circus that is run by Dream Travelers and features real magic—mysterious events start happening. The once orderly grounds of the circus become riddled with hidden threats. And the ringmaster realizes not only are his circus and its magic at risk, but also his very life.

Vagabond Circus caters to the skeptics. Without skeptics, it would close its doors. This is because Vagabond Circus runs for two reasons and only two reasons: first and foremost to provide the lost and lonely Dream Travelers a place to be illustrious. And secondly, to show the nonbelievers that there's still magic in the world. If they believe, then they care, and if they care, then they don't destroy. They stop the small abuse that day-by-day breaks down humanity's spirit. If Vagabond Circus makes one skeptic believe in magic, then they halt the cycle, just a little bit. They allow a little more love into this world. That's Dr. Dave Raydon's mission. And that's why this ringmaster recruits. That's why he directs. That's why he puts on a show that makes people question their beliefs. He wants the world to believe in magic once again.

Paralyzed, #2
Released, #3

Ren Series:

Ren: The Man Behind the Monster, #1:
Born with the power to control minds, hypnotize others, and read thoughts, Ren Lewis, is certain of one thing: God made a mistake. No one should be born with so much power. A monster awoke in him the same year he received his gifts. At ten years old. A prepubescent boy with the ability to control others might merely abuse his powers, but Ren allowed it to corrupt him. And since he can have and do anything he wants, Ren should be happy. However, his journey teaches him that harboring so much power doesn't bring happiness, it steals it. Once this realization sets in, Ren makes up his mind to do the one thing that can bring his tortured soul some peace. He must kill the monster.

Note This book is NA and has strong language, violence and sexual references.

Ren: God's Little Monster, #2
Ren: The Monster Inside the Monster, #3
Ren: The Monster's Adventure, #3.5
Ren: The Monster's Death

Olento Research Series:

Alpha Wolf, #1:
Twelve men went missing.

Six months later they awake from drug-induced stupors to find themselves locked in a lab.

And on the night of a new moon, eleven of those men, possessed by new—and inhuman—powers, break out of their prison and race through the streets of Los Angeles until they disappear one by one into the night.

Olento Research wants its experiments back. Its CEO, Mika Lenna, will tear every city apart until he has his werewolves imprisoned once again. He didn't undertake a huge risk just to lose his would-be assassins.

However, the Lucidite Institute's main mission is to save the world from injustices. Now, it's Adelaide's job to find these mutated men and protect them and society, and fast. Already around the nation, wolflike men are being spotted. Attacks on innocent women are happening. And then, Adelaide realizes what her next step must be: She has to find the alpha wolf first. Only once she's located him can she stop whoever is behind this experiment to create wild beasts out of human beings.

Lone Wolf, #2
Rabid Wolf, #3
Bad Wolf, #4

CONNECT WITH THE AUTHORS

Connect with Sarah and sign up for her email list here:

http://www.sarahnoffke.com/connect/

Michael Anderle Social

Website: http://lmbpn.com

Email List: http://lmbpn.com/email/

Social Media:

https://www.facebook.com/LMBPNPublishing

https://twitter.com/MichaelAnderle

https://www.instagram.com/lmbpn_publishing/

https://www.bookbub.com/authors/michael-anderle